711743

W9-CBK-538

COLD SKIN

cold skin

Steven Herrick

FRONT STREET
Honesdale, Pennsylvania

Also by Steven Herrick

By the River

Naked Bunyip Dancing

The Wolf

Originally published in Australia by Allen & Unwin, 2007

Printed in the United States of America
Designed by Helen Robinson
First U.S. edition, 2009
Second printing

Library of Congress Cataloging-in-Publication Data
Herrick, Steven.
Cold skin / Steven Herrick. — 1st U.S. ed.
p. cm.
Summary: In a rural Australian coal mining town shortly
after World War II, teenaged Eddie makes a startling discovery
when he investigates the murder of a local high school girl.

ISBN 978-1-59078-572-0 (hardcover : alk. paper)

[1. Novels in verse. 2. Country life—Australia—Fiction.
3. Murder—Fiction. 4. Fathers and sons—Fiction.
5. Australia—History—20th century—Fiction.
6. Mystery and detective stories.] I. Title.

PZ7.5.H47Co 2009
[Fic]—dc22
2008018620

FRONT STREET
An Imprint of Boyds Mills Press, Inc.
815 Church Street
Honesdale, Pennsylvania 18431

COLD SKIN

Characters

Eddie Holding

Larry Holding

Albert Holding

Sally Holmes

Colleen O'Connor

Mayor Paley

Mr. Carter

Sergeant Grainer

Mr. Butcher

Contents

ONE

A Bright Future

Eddie Holding

They named me Eddie
after Mum's father,
who died before I was born.
"A quiet, stubborn bastard,"
says my dad.
I'm not sure if he's talking about
Grandad or me.
We live near the railway tracks
beside the Jamison River,
two miles out of town,
opposite the slag heap,
overgrown with thistles
and yellow dandelions.
Dad and me and my brother Larry
built our place in a real hurry
'cause we had nowhere else to live
after Grandma died
and the Wilsons took her house
before we'd had a fair chance
to say good-bye to Gran's memories.
They said it was their house
and I guess it was
because they went out and sold it.
So we packed everything on
Mr. Laycock's Leyland truck
and drove it here,
where we bought some land,

no bigger than an acre,
with the last of Dad's army pay.
Larry and me set to work
dragging logs from the bush
with our horse.
Dad mixed concrete
and poured the foundation
in the hot sun
while Mum washed our clothes in the old tub,
hanging them over the wire
stretched between two poles
along the boundary to our yard.
We lived in a tent
loaned from Mr. Paley, the mayor.
He said,
"Anything for a supporter."
And for six weeks
me and Larry didn't go to school.
We built this three-room log house
that looks like a squat brown toad
sitting on a rise
about to jump into the Jamison River.

Eddie

Taylors Bend is named after a bloke
who owned some of this valley a long time ago.
Mr. Taylor lost his sons in the Great War,
and all he had left
was a few hundred head of sheep
and the river that flooded his fields most winters.
They say when his sons didn't come home,
he tied himself to a tractor wheel
and jumped into the water at the deepest part.
No one could find his body,
so they named this bend to remember him.

It's the best place for skimming stones.
You can dig your toes deep into the sand.
Once I skipped a flat black rock
fair to the sandstone wall
on the far side of the river.
I'm fishing for yabbies
because Mum says
there's only potatoes to eat tonight.
So I tie the pork fat to the string
and toss it in,
waiting for the tug.
Sometimes I catch ten river yabbies
with the same piece of meat.
Into the old tin bucket they go,
half-full of river water,

ready for Mum to boil 'em up.
We have them with spuds
cooked slow in our wood oven,
so you can taste the smoke.
Larry whispers to me,
"Blackfella food.
That's what you're eating."
I don't care what color eats the yabbies.
It don't make them taste any less sweet.
I say,
"Good food, Larry.
Fresh-caught food."
He don't know what he's got.
My smart lazy brother.

Albert Holding

I came home from the army
and saw my wife and two sons
standing on the train platform,
waiting for me to hug them.
I'd been away too long,
even if it was only driving transport
across the desert in the Territory,
while other blokes died of starvation and malaria
and God knows what else,
a few thousand miles north.
The closest I got to war
was loading the heavy artillery
onto the ships in Darwin Harbor
and getting into fights at the pub
with the blokes from the navy,
who could swing a fist as sure as a pint.
I drove the bloody trucks
such long nights across the country
with only Corporal Cheetham for company.
Cheetham had a fine way of spitting
between his teeth,
scratching his head,
and saying, "Well, bugger me"
whenever we got a flat tire
out there in the middle of nowhere.
We'd sit under the cold stars
and wait for daylight before changing the tire,

rather than struggling around in the dark.
I'd stand on the dirt track
and smoke cigarette after cigarette,
not saying much.
That's how I spent the war.
When it was all over, after demobilization,
fresh-faced girls in the city had welcome smiles
and kisses for every man in a uniform.
I walked to the train station,
dizzy with the smell of perfume and victory.
We all came home on a slow train,
sharing jokes and beers,
playing cards
and telling long-winded stories
of what we'd do once we got back.
Then I saw my family on the platform.
My wife with her black hair
covered in a scarf with yellow sunflowers.
Larry shuffling his feet in the dirt,
his hands deep in his pockets.
And Eddie waving, smiling,
saying, "Hello. Welcome back."
to each of the men
as they stepped from the carriage.
My family.
"Well, bugger me."

Eddie

"Welcome to a big year for Burruga,"
says Mr. Paley, our mayor.
He's standing on the speaker's box
at the rotunda in Memorial Park,
waving his hat above his head
as he calls to everyone gathered.
"Rally around, ladies and gentlemen.
I'm going to put our town on the map.
Imagine, a modern blast furnace near the coal mine
and a new ticket office for the railway station."
He points toward the jerry-built shack opposite
and wipes the sweat from his brow
with a white handkerchief
flourished from the breast pocket of his suit.
He leans forward and says,
"And, ladies,
I promise a new haberdashery
for my department store.
An emporium of taste and refinement.
Something special for all of you."
Mr. Paley winks at Mrs. Blythe and Mrs. Reynolds.
Both smile and bow their heads slightly.
"Let's put the war behind us
and build for the future."
As he says this he raises both hands into the air,
clenching his fists in triumph.
Mr. Wright, the mine manager, steps forward

and starts up a three-cheers for the mayor.
He calls to the crowd,
"Mayor Paley, a man of will and purpose."

Me and Dad walk home from the park.
Dad brushes the flies from his face
and drags hard on his smoke.
"What does Paley know about the war?
That fat bastard stayed home,
cowering in his father's store.
'Will and purpose.'
Yeah. He *will* get richer on *purpose*."
Mr. Paley is still chatting to the ladies
on the stairs of the rotunda.
He stands one step higher than everyone else,
his voice booming over their heads.
"A bright future.
I promise."

Eddie

The coal mine is surrounded
by a high wire fence.
In the far corner I scrape the loose dirt
from under the boundary
until there's enough space to lie on my back
and pull myself under the wire.
Through the gritty window of the rusted tin shed
I can see the picks, shovels, and lanterns
stored neatly on wooden shelves.
Dad hates me talking about the mine,
and he made me repeat this year in school
just to stop me from working underground.
I'm stronger and taller than him.
I weigh close on twelve stone
and most of it's muscle.
I can move rocks
bigger than a yard square,
and I can swing an ax to split firewood
quicker than Larry.
You can load my arms with ironbark
and I'll carry it all inside,
no problem.
This mine is where I want to be,
with the returned soldiers
and my mates from school,
who earn a decent wage doing a real job.

I dodge between the outbuildings
to watch the men in their dirt-colored overalls
and thick brown boots
prepare for the night shift,
laughing and singing
like they're going out to the pub.
They strap their helmets on,
test the light, twice, for safety,
and clip the strap tight under their chin.
I want to sneak in behind them
and take the trolley ride
down into the soul of the world
and see what it's like,
deep in the pit
where muscle and rock
fight their daily battle.

Albert Holding

You can smell the coal smoke
long before the train rounds the bend
and drops down into the narrow valley.
Some days in winter the plume settles so low
you could stand on Jaspers Hill
and not know there's a town below.
Let me tell you, I was grateful
that scabby bastard Wilson evicted us.
The land we bought is next to useless,
but at least it's out of town.
The wind blows the smoke east
back up through Dulwich Gap.
At least a man can breathe in his own backyard.
Not like the miners
who walk through town to work at the pit.
My mates, every one of them.
I remember marching in our khaki uniforms,
wheeling down Main Street in perfect file
while the town,
the whole district,
cheered us on and waved little flags.
The chin strap on the slouch hat
kept our eyes straight
should we be tempted to gaze at all the young sheilas
smiling and waving our way.
That was at the start of the war.
The high and mighty ladies at Paley's

go on about us living out here like gypsies.

We're only one rung above Barney Haggerty,

who sleeps in a cave halfway up the gap,

drunk most of the time.

They don't know what he went through during the war.

They certainly know sod-all about me.

And I want to keep it that way.

Eddie

Dad says it's not right,

working on Laycock's farm.

He didn't fight a war

to muck out after ignorant animals.

Hay bailing,

picking eggs,

slopping out pig swill.

That's work for a boy, he says.

But Mr. Laycock's got no kids

and no one wants the job,

not when there's men's work to be done.

When I bring up the mine again,

Dad slams his fists on the table

and shouts,

"I ain't going underground.

And neither are you, boy.

Not while you live in my house."

I want to tell him it's our house.

We helped build it.

But most of all,

I want to ask him

why he's always so angry.

Ever since he got home,

he's been blaming me and Larry for everything

when we done nothing wrong.

"The mine needs workers, Dad.

I'm not doing much at school

except wasting time."
He shakes his head
before walking outside,
muttering,
"I'm better off with the pigs."

Larry Holding

My big brother's not too smart.
He thinks living out here,
miles from anyone,
is an adventure.
I heard him say that.
"An adventure."
Shooting rabbits for dinner
with our rusty-barreled .22,
picking blackberries for supper,
fishing in the river
with a string line tied to bamboo,
hoping for a silver eel
so Mum can make an evil-smelling stew.
This is my brother and his life.
This is why I want to shoot through.
But you don't leave Burruga,
not without an education,
even I know that.
So I don't want to miss school.
In the baking-hot classroom of Burruga Central,
I listen to Mr. Butcher
with his math and stupid algebra
and his splitting infinitives in English,
whatever they're meant to be.
I keep a clean book
with lines straight
and practice handwriting that slopes

"like a long-haired girl dancing,"
Butcher says in his nancy-voice.
But here's my deal:
the pact I made with myself—
I'll give it a burl
and do every inch of Butcher's homework
if only I can leave town when I'm fifteen,
in six months' time,
after the exams,
after I get the certificate.
I'm going to wave it in their faces and say,
"See ya.
See ya forever."

Mayor Paley

I tell them exactly what they want to hear,
and I'll try to make it happen, truly.
Everyone in town should have a job.
We're sitting on a pile of coal here.
So I promise what I can,
and now it just depends on money
and the state government.
Most of these people don't realize
it isn't the town that's building the things I promise.
It's the state.
I'll do my best to swing it, I will.
A man of my stature has influence.
And friends.
Trust me.
It'll take a few trips to the city, mind you,
and I'll have to spend some town money
entertaining those business folk
so they're sure we're worth helping,
way out here.
But I know a few people,
associates of my father.
Good citizens.
Rich people in the city.
I will never cease working for my town.
"Will and purpose."
Mr. Wright spoke the truth.

Albert Holding

Fatty Paley was a sneaky kid in baggy trousers
with a limp
and a father who owned the general store.
And Fatty grows into,
expands into,
the mayor of this town,
while the rest of us are fighting the war.
Driving trucks *is* fighting a war.
Fatty charms the ladies
with his boarding-school education
and his prissy sincere voice.
He greased the palms of certain people
who backed him as mayor
while the rest of us were thousands of miles away.
Fatty gets fatter and richer than his old man,
and he has a sign above his store,
his crummy little general store,
that reads Paley's Emporium,
because Fatty's too proud to own just a shop.
And he had the hide to stand on the platform
when our train came in,
holding out his arms,
hugging,
yeah, hugging,
every man who came home from the war.
It made my flesh creep.

Eddie

I'm not much good at math
and
I'm not much good at grammar
and
I'm not much good at geography
and
I'm not much good at anything,
says Mr. Butcher
with his hair slicked back so tight
it draws the blood from his face.
His thick black-rimmed glasses
sit useless on his nose
as he stands at the chalkboard
tapping his long ruler,
talking to the class,
pointing at a map of the world,
and trying to convince us
our country is the biggest island
in the whole world.
I believe him,
it's just the idea of an island,
you know,
surrounded by water,
when it looks to me that map shows
nearly every country is surrounded by water.
So I put up my hand and say,
"Africa looks bigger than Australia, sir."

Mr. Butcher removes his glasses,
rolls his eyes, and slowly shakes his head.
"Yes, Eddie Holding.
But Africa is a *continent,*
not a country.
Didn't I mention that?"
He says it like he *did* mention that,
but I can't remember,
and judging by the look on everyone else's face,
they can't remember either.
Continent.
Country.
So Mr. Butcher explains the difference,
and I can tell he's mad at me
because I picked him up on something.
After he's finished he's says his usual
"There, Eddie.
You're not much good at geography.
You're not much good at remembering."

I see Larry smirking
and hear the giggles from behind me,
so I stand up,
wave my arm just like Mr. Butcher
and say,
"And you're not much good at teaching, sir."
Then I walk out of the classroom
and head to Jamison River to go swimming.
I'm very good at swimming.

I reckon the river
and the sunny day
are worth the punishment I'm in for
on Monday morning.

Larry

My stupid brother can't keep his mouth shut.
Yeah, Butcher never told us about continents.
In all the years pointing at that boring map.
I know he never told us because, unlike Eddie,
I remember everything I'm taught,
and I studied it in the library,
tracing my finger over the world atlas,
imagining how long it'll take me
to travel the distance from here to all those places.
Eddie will get six cuts on Monday,
and we'll all be given a lecture
with Butcher's voice like power lines in winter,
whining in the wind.
You're never sure if they'll snap over your head.
He'll go on about manners,
proper behavior,
respect for your elders,
and I'll be thinking,
just get on with it, Butcher,
and whip my stupid brother a few times
with your nasty little cane.
Let's start algebra because I still don't understand it all
and I've only got six months more
and yes, you are a hopeless teacher,
but you're the only teacher we got,
so get on with it.

Eddie

Sally Holmes runs through the willows
and stands beside me, looking down at the river.
"As soon as the bell went
I was out of there like a shot."
She kicks off her shoes,
flings her socks after them,
not taking her eyes off the clear water
and the rope dangling from the river gum tree.
"Do you think I can grab it, first go?"
Sally orders me to look away,
and I hear the rustle of her dress
as she pulls it over her shoulders.
She's wearing dark blue swimmers
and I feel my face go blush red
as I try my best not to look at her.
"I'll go first, if you want, Sally.
It's going to be freezing."
She has wavy hair like flowing cream,
and she's as tall as me,
with long legs and a narrow waist.
I love Sally,
but I don't tell anyone that,
especially not Sally.
I'm her friend,
and I listen to her wild laughter
as she runs from the bank
and leaps toward the rope,

both hands grabbing the very end
as she swings far out to midstream and hangs there,
looking back at me,
"Too late, Eddie!"
She falls with a scream,
hits the water in a curled-up ball,
comes up laughing and hooting,
racing back to shore to do it all again.
She pushes her hair back
and flicks her wet hands,
spraying cold drops all over me.
"Come on, jump in.
It's not too chilly."
I hold the rope for her
because if there's one thing I like
more than swimming,
it's watching beautiful Sally Holmes
laughing and rope-swinging.
Just me and her in the afternoon
at Jamison River.

Sally Holmes

All the wowsers and bulletheads
in school say Eddie is slow.
They call him names behind his back.
"Pudding brain" and "clod boy."
They say it quietly,
because whether he is or not
doesn't matter so much,
they know that if he ever heard them
there'd be trouble—
trouble in the form of big Eddie
and his oversized fists.

They're all wrong anyway.
I know Eddie better than they do.
He'd never hurt anyone,
not unless they meant him harm.
We swim down at the waterhole,
even in winter when there's no one else around.
One day I'm going to dive deep enough
to touch the bottom,
way out in the middle of the river.
Eddie calls this place Sally's Spot in my honor.
He holds the rope for me,
hands me my towel.
He's a gentleman,
he's my friend.

Eddie

I found the necklace beside the train tracks
and knew that someone rich
and spoiled,
or angry,
had thrown it from the train window.
It shone in the grass,
and I rushed across the line to pick it up
and polish its shiny-metal smoothness.
I opened the heart-shaped locket.
The inscription read
To My Beloved.
That's all.
No signature.
Maybe he was embarrassed to sign his name.
Or he didn't mean it,
didn't have the guts to commit.
Perhaps that's why it got tossed by a girl
who couldn't stand to wear it around her neck
and be reminded of his lies.
When I got home
I hid it in my drawer,
stuffed in the oldest pair of socks.
For safekeeping.
For Sally.

Sally

I don't know what came over me.
When Eddie held the rope
as I walked toward him,
dripping wet and trembling from the cold water,
well,
when he handed me the rope
and smiled in his relaxed way,
I leaned forward and kissed him.
On the lips.
I closed my eyes,
and I'm sure he closed his.
We stood there together
with our lips touching
for a few seconds,
and I stopped shaking.
I gripped the rope tightly
as I drifted back from Eddie
and flung myself
as far into the river
as the swing would take me,
and just before I dropped
I looked back toward the bank.
Eddie was gone.

Eddie

Sally has a tiny gap between her two front teeth.
I get lost in her smile.
That's what I was looking at
when she walked up to me
all wet and shivering,
and I wasn't ready for what she did.
Bloody hell.
Would I ever be ready?

At school, when it comes to Friday games,
like tug-of-war,
I'm the first picked,
and the other side always asks for an extra player.
When deliveries come in from the city,
they get me to unload the truck
and I toss the boxes into the storeroom.
Sometimes I lift three at a time
just to see how much I can carry.
I tell the driver this is better than schoolwork.

Nobody in school is stronger than me.
But when Sally Holmes kissed me,
I never felt so weak in all my life.

Eddie

I do the washing up for Mum
same as every night,
because Larry says he has to study.
Aren't we in the same class?
Don't we do the same homework?
Larry sneers when I say this.
"My homework is nothing like yours."
I know what he means,
but I don't argue
because someone's got to do the dishes
for Mum,
who's done all the cooking.
Tonight I wash real slow
because I'm looking out the window
down to Jamison River
and I'm thinking of Sally Holmes
with her red lips wet,
brushing mine,
and I figure
it's worth it
in my little life
to stand here
dreaming.

Larry

Yeah, my brother
hangs around with Sally,
but I reckon
she's just taking pity on him,
on account of her too-good ways.
I don't care.
She ain't that pretty.
Give me Colleen O'Connor any day.
She's as attractive as any movie star, I reckon.
That's why every morning
I go to the library
and sit at the same desk as Colleen.
She don't say much,
but I don't care
because I work on reading my book
and looking at her white blouse
and imagining what's underneath.
I'm getting so good at it,
sometimes
when the bell rings
I can't move for a few minutes
until it's safe to stand,
if you know what I mean.
I watch Colleen walk out of the library,
her fine legs and ankles,
and I sit here
getting the courage

to ask her out,
one day,
when I think the time is right.
Me and Colleen.

Eddie

In the backyard of our old house, before the war,
Dad built us a cubby
out of cast-off fence posts and rusty nails.
Me and Larry would play in it most of the weekend,
pretending to be cowboy scouts
waiting for the Indians to attack.
Dad carved us guns out of pinewood
and colored the barrels with charcoal,
drilling a hole where the trigger should be.
He taught us how to twirl the six-gun.
Me and Larry would face off across the grass
until Dad called "shoot."
We'd both fling ourselves to the ground,
pointing the guns at each other,
yelling "bang, bang, bang"
until Dad would wink at one of us to play dead.
He did it in turn so Larry and me
each got to blow imaginary smoke from our barrels
and be a Western hero
while Dad carried off the body of our brother
to the far corner of the yard
where the compost heap steamed.
Dad called it Tombstone Hill.
That was when we were young.
Before Dad signed up for the war.
Long before the war.

TWO | # Coal Town

Mr. Butcher

I have ambitions
for teaching in the city.
At a grammar school,
where everyone,
I mean everyone,
addresses you as "sir."
Where they have servants
preparing lunch for staff,
served in a dining room lined with pictures
of the school history.
They have linen on the tables,
leather chairs,
and the only sound you hear
is the clink of fine bone china.
A school where you can dedicate your life
and become a history master.
And the students sit up straight
in spotless, pressed uniforms,
listening.
And they all have plans.
Solicitors.
Doctors.
Managers.
A school where they play rugby,
serve tea and scones
on the sidelines every Saturday,
with the parents asking after "young Harold"

and whether his homework
is up to standard.
As if it isn't anything but perfect.
Mr. Butcher.
Master Butcher.
Sir.

Mr. Butcher

I stroll to school down Main Street,
listening to the groaning freight train
pulling the night-shift coal load to the coast.
I nod to Calder, the butcher,
and Old Man Wilson,
who runs the hardware.
He spends most of his day
sitting in his office,
looking down on the store
as he sips his tea
and watches each customer,
tipping his hat to the ladies
but rarely getting up from his
expensive swivel chair,
letting his son do the work.
I say "good morning" to Mr. Carter,
editor of the *Guardian,*
who keeps an eagle eye
on Main Street early morning,
as if the news is just waiting to happen
outside his shop front.
Mrs. Kain sits on her bentwood chair
at the front of Sunset Café,
having her first tea of the day.
She calls to her husband,
"Is the grill ready yet, Ernie?"
I raise my hat and keep walking to the corner,

past Paley's Emporium,
with the staff already busy
sweeping and dusting
because Paley doesn't employ cleaners.
He gets the staff to do everything.

Mr. Carter

I've had some front-page stories,
let me tell you.
Our boys marching to war in crisp uniforms,
eyes forward,
the click of heels down Main Street.
The day our football team won the Shield
for the first time in a generation, by Jove.
They mounted the trophy in the window at Paley's,
and the young children stood admiring it till sunset.
The collapse of number 2 shaft
at the end of the day shift.
A pall of dust settled over the town
while we waited for the bodies to be brought up.
The following Sunday the church was full
for the first time in years.
A week later, Mayor Paley unveiled the memorial
for two family men lost.
In the paper the next day
was a photo of the grieving miners,
arm in arm at the ceremony.
I gave a paragraph to Paley's speech.
The rest of the page was devoted
to the brave souls lost
and the Union Appeal for their families
with an anonymous one-hundred-pound donation
to get things moving.
Never you mind who it was.

I'm careful with what I put on the front page.

No rubbish or gossip.

I don't print what people think,

only what they say.

If they say it, I quote them.

I've studied awhile on who to believe in town

and how to check on those I don't.

I run a newspaper,

not the town diary.

And those who don't like it,

well,

they can listen to the gossips

at Paley's store.

Mayor Paley

Dr. Barnes said it was "fluid on the knee,"
and he wrote a letter to the army,
dismissing my chances of serving.
I wanted to enlist.
I craved to go with the rest of the men.
But, my knee.
It was cruel to watch them leave.
I made a rousing speech at the farewell parade
and decided to serve at home.
I ran for mayor to improve my town.
Not for myself.
Lord.
Didn't I already have enough to do with my store?
But we all must make sacrifices,
and so I put my name forward
and won.
In a landslide.

It's the fluid that makes me limp,
but I don't complain,
even when a youngster from school,
some little tyke, asks me,
"Did you get that in the war?"
Bloody cheeky kid.
No respect for my efforts.
I do it all for this town.

Mayor Paley

I didn't approve of what Carter wrote
when I was elected mayor.
He didn't have to print "unopposed"
as the headline,
implying that there was no one else to vote for.
I was elected because of what I stood for,
what I had to offer,
because the whole town,
all the women
and the men not at war,
everyone believed in me.
I call that a landslide.

A lesser man would have canceled
all advertisements from the paper
in protest.
But I like to think of myself as a big man,
a trifle overweight,
but big in spirit and generosity.
I don't have much time for the likes of Carter.
My father always said
to remember your enemies
as well as your friends,
and don't trust either of them.

Mr. Carter

Mr. Butcher walks by each day
with a shallow "good morning."
That's all.
He thinks I'm looking for a front page.
Tell me,
how can a man employed as a teacher
be so clueless?
What I am doing is watching the kids
wandering ragtag to school,
and even though I dare not,
I'm writing their stories.
The freckle-faced boys,
future miners.
In five years' time I'll be nodding to them
as they come coughing up Main Street.
A few will leave town to work in the city,
in an office,
with clean clothes
and a determination to forget
where they came from.
The rest will bide their time on farms
or in the shops in town.
Some of the girls will fall pregnant,
choosing their life
by what goes on down by the river
one Saturday night.
Except Sally Holmes

and Colleen O'Connor.
Those two,
they'll make their way.
They won't let Butcher's pedestrian teaching
ruin their chances.

So I answer Mr. Butcher with a firm nod,
and I keep vigil on those two girls
because I know
there's always hope.

Sally

This morning I see Eddie
taking the shortcut to school,
along the riverbank.
He swings his bag from side to side,
hand to hand,
playing some intricate game only he knows.
I wolf-whistle as loud as I dare
and quickly duck behind a bush.
Eddie stops and looks around,
the hint of a smile on his face.
When he starts walking away,
I try to whistle again
but nothing comes except laughter.
He's seen me!
I grab my bag and run to meet him.
He's carrying a sprig of mountain wattle
and he offers it to me.
I push the stalk into my top buttonhole.
"Thanks, Eddie."
He smiles back,
and I'm pretty sure
we're both thinking of what happened by the river,
even though neither of us is going to say
a word about it,
today,
or the day after.

Colleen O'Connor

Larry scares me with his wandering eyes
and greasy hair.
I know he's looking at me,
sitting across the desk every morning
in the library.
I wish there was somewhere else to sit
but I need a desk to finish my homework
and the library is the only room open before bell.
So I focus really hard on what I'm doing,
and I only say "morning" to Larry
and go straight back to work.
Why doesn't he go out to the veranda
where all the other girls are,
chatting, flirting, laughing,
and leave me to study?
I don't give him time to start anything.
I'm not stupid.
I've learned enough about boys
to know you give them an inch,
well, they'll take more than a mile.
And Larry, he's the type who'd enjoy
telling the whole town all about it.
That's not happening to me.
Mum says I'm too good for Burruga.
I take one quick look at Larry
and think she may be right.

Eddie

I hate Monday mornings.
Mr. Butcher is staring out the window,
and the whole class keeps quiet,
trying not to disturb him.
But there's no way I can do this algebra
without help,
so I risk it.
I raise my hand,
swollen
from his cane an hour ago,
and wait,
hoping he'll see,
but he's paying no attention to us.
So I cough, too loudly.
He rises from his chair and smirks.
"Don't grunt, Holding.
Speak up if you need help."
Some of the class giggle,
and Mr. Butcher looks pleased with himself,
so I forget algebra and say,
"No need for help, sir.
I just want to go to the toilet."
The class sniggers again,
only this time Butcher's not sure
if they're laughing with him
or at him.
He looks at me for a long time,

adjusting his glasses,

"When it comes to algebra, Holding,

you have the intellectual capacity of a newt."

I clench my fists under the desk.

"Even newts need to go to the dunny, sir."

Everyone laughs.

Butcher's eyes flash.

He stands quickly and points outside.

That means I can go.

I walk slowly,

smiling,

knowing he'll be looking for payback

sometime today.

Eddie

After the river kiss,
Sally and me seem closer.
No, I'm not imagining it.
We sit together at lunch
and she tells me where she's planning to go
when she leaves school
in exactly five months
and fifteen days.
That makes me sad.
I try not to show it,
but if Sally leaves Burruga
then I know I'll be alone.
Better to let the mine swallow me
than stay in school without her.
I decide to make the most of the time we got left
before she gets too big for this small town.
But I know she's already stepping on that train,
and I'm waving from the platform,
cursing under my breath …
the necklace still in my pocket.

Albert Holding

Every Friday
I stump work early
so as to get to the pub
with a few hours of drinking time left.
The wife complains when I stagger home.
Reckons I'm roaring drunk.
So what?
A bloke needs some relief after
a week of feeding chooks,
mucking out pigs,
and running errands for Mrs. Laycock,
who's too crook to move from the veranda.
She spends her day watching me work,
waiting for her husband
to come home from plowing the far paddock.
So I have a drink after work
with some buddies from town
and listen to their stories of the mine.
The stink of coal dust clings to their clothes,
their skin and hair.
The only job worse than Laycock's
is the one underground.
We all get merry together
and tell lies about the war
and lewd stories about women
we dreamed of meeting,
fighting far from Burruga.

Frank O'Connor offers the shout,

and we all accept

because Frank spent time in Burma

and whatever he saw

he keeps close to his chest.

So we all tell jokes,

as rude as possible,

to help him forget,

to help us all forget,

even those of us with bugger all to remember.

Albert Holding

I'm standing at the bar,

bending my elbow,

listening to Donald Cheetham tell his lies,

when Fatty Paley comes in,

taking up way too much space

with his back-slapping

and his toady voice.

He bowls up to the bar and trumpets,

"A round on me for everyone.

For my mates."

I force a smile,

take his beer,

swear under my breath,

and scull it in one gulp,

glad to be done with it.

Fatty stands next to Frank

and offers him another.

Oily bastard.

Frank's had enough to cope with.

The jungle,

the Japs,

and now Fatty.

Colleen

When I'm walking down Main Street after school,
I see the miners coming toward me
in their coal-dirt overalls.
Their teeth shine through smeared faces.
They're laughing and joking around,
and someone always shouts,
"How ya goin', blondie?"
I can feel their eyes on me.
The Johnston boys look quite handsome,
even in dusty overalls.
My dad walks with them and nods at me.
He tells me they're good blokes,
just having a laugh.
And Mum says they look at me
because I'm pretty.
I suppose I am.
She says
that their eyes
and their stares
are the price I pay.
I've just got to keep my head high
and my eyes forward.
Easier said than done.
But when Les Johnston winks at me,
I smile back,
careful not to let Dad see.
Les is six feet tall

and his hair is dark and wavy,
and a girl wouldn't mind
running her fingers through it,
given half a chance.
One day.

Larry

Yeah, I nicked the beer
from behind the Railway Hotel
and I sit in Memorial Park knocking back a few.
Eddie walks by,
looking like he's got somewhere to go.
"Hey, brother. Come here."
He turns and waves,
checking both ways before walking across the grass.
"No one will see, Eddie.
Here, have a drink."
He steps back as if I've got some disease.
"Geez, it's beer, not cyanide."
He's not going to take it.
Be blowed if he's not!
"Eddie. Catch!"
He doesn't spill a drop,
grabbing it in both hands,
wondering what to do next.
He has a quick sip
before handing it back.
"That wasn't so bad, was it?"
He sits beside me
and shakes his head.
"You're a talkative bastard, Eddie."
He grins slowly and says,
"Just like our father."
"Don't remind me," I say.

"The grumpy bugger's always on my case."

Eddie reaches for the beer

and takes a long swig.

"He wasn't always like that, Larry."

He wipes the mouth of the bottle

before handing it back.

"Yeah, yeah. I know.

The bloody war.

Except the old bastard didn't go anywhere.

Just chased his tail around the desert.

He's hardly a hero."

Eddie nods and says,

"I gotta go, Larry.

Don't let Sergeant Grainger catch you."

He walks off down the street,

his hands deep in his pockets.

Mayor Paley

It's just a little treat
for the men of my town.
They deserve a beer.
Even lazy beggars
like Albert Holding
who won't work in the mine.
He wastes his days
gathering eggs and feeding cows
like some novice farm boy.
Hell,
I don't care
as long as they vote for me
next election.
I down a few pots myself,
to show I'm one of them,
even if I'm better educated
and wear tailored clothes
and own a few places around town.
I don't ever mention that.
It's not good form.
That Holding fellow
didn't even thank me for his beer.
Ungrateful boor.
I force a laugh
and slap him on the back
to show I'm the bigger man.

Sally

Dad meets me at netball.
He's there, regular as clockwork,
a few minutes before we finish,
as the sun fades behind Jaspers Hill.
He hates Friday evenings.
"The drunk night," he calls it.
And even though it's only
a few blocks to our house,
he won't let me walk it alone.
He always invites Jean Bennett
to come with us
because she lives on the way
and he's not letting her walk home alone either.
The men are still at the pub,
getting the last few drinks in before closing.
My dad won't take no for an answer,
and every Friday I see him
looking at the girls strolling home
in the opposite direction
and I know he hates that.
He doesn't say much on the walk.
He's thinking of the other girls
and their fathers jostling each other at the pub,
trying to get one last shout
before the publican calls time
and they all stagger out,
wondering which way is home.

Larry

I stand the empty bottle below the plaque
dedicated to the soldiers from the Great War.
"Sorry, fellas."
Jamming the head of my next bottle
under the brass plate,
I twist and the cap snaps off,
rolling along the concrete like a stray dice.
There's nothing to do now
except wander down Princess Street
toward the river.
Trying my best to follow the white line,
not having much luck though.
The bastard who painted this
must have been drunk.
A dog starts barking
and jumping against his lead.
I'm tempted to chuck the bottle at it,
except there's still some left
and I'm not wasting it on no stupid animal.
At the end of the street
I climb the fence and cut myself on the barbed-wire.
What idiot fences off the river,
for God's sake?
I hurl the bottle across the water,
smashing it on the rocks.
"Better not swim there, children."
At least it's quiet down here,

away from all the old men wandering home,
singing tunes from the war
and vomiting in the gutters.
My head is spinning.
Must be Mum's awful cooking.

Mr. Butcher

On Friday evenings
I take my supper
at the Sunset Café.
A mixed grill
with Mr. Kain's special:
grilled mince rolled into a long thin sausage,
cooked with tomatoes and mushrooms.
He makes it for me alone
because no one else in this town
cares much about food on Friday night.
I ignore the noise from the pub.
A mob of uncouth drunks falling about,
spilling drinks and cursing.
Mrs. Kain pours me another cup
of her strong black tea.
"Off to visit your mother again, Mr. Butcher?"
Forcing a smile, I answer,
"Dear Mrs. Kain,
My poor mother insists she can cope alone.
But—"
Mrs. Kain interrupts,
"You're a good man, Mr. Butcher.
A good man."

In a few hours
I'll be on the train
heading into the city,

away from this backwater,

to spend two days

and my wage

on pleasures you can't enjoy in this town.

Delights that I deserve

after another week

teaching the unteachable.

Things that a single man needs

when he lives in a town of married old matrons

and young schoolgirls.

Things that Mrs. Kain and my mother,

dead for ten long years,

wouldn't understand.

Things that make me forget

Monday morning.

Eddie

I dangle my legs over a fork in the branch
of the old fig tree,
waiting for the night train to the city.
A lady beetle lands on my arm
and tickles along my skin.
Mr. Butcher takes a long time to light his pipe.
He stands at the far end of the platform,
away from the lights,
thinking no one sees him.
I do.
Maybe he has a wife and kids in the city,
where he goes every weekend,
but I don't believe it.
He's not the type.
The train whistle echoes through Dulwich Gap.
Mr. Butcher empties his pipe onto the tracks
and tucks it into his overcoat.
He glances up and down the platform,
picks up his Gladstone bag,
and pulls his hat low over his eyes.
I see you, Mr. Butcher.
I see you.

Mr. Carter

Here comes Larry Holding
staggering toward my office,
doing his best to stay upright,
talking to some imaginary friend
who dances around him.
A slow waltz, by the look of things.

When the paper is put to bed,
I relax with a cup of tea
on the old lounge chair
in the front room,
with all the lights out.
It's then I watch my town lurch by,
getting itself into such a tangle.

Larry wants to fight the lamppost.
He's so drunk
he starts swearing at it.
I expect he'll throw the first punch.
My money's on the lamppost.
He sits in the gutter for a while,
scratching his head,
shaking his fist at the post
and muttering to himself.
Maybe his imaginary friend
became bored and moved on.
Larry gradually stands and sways

before wandering off
slowly down the street.
There's no pedigree in that family.
A dad with a chip on his shoulder,
brooding on Laycock's farm.
A mum, quiet as a dormouse,
sending the boys out to find food at the river
or shoot rabbits on Jaspers Hill.
And big Eddie,
stuck at school
when he really wants to work those muscles
where they might be of some use.

Larry

They shouldn't stick lampposts
right on the footpath
where you can walk into them.
If only I had an ax.
Hang on,
Colleen's house isn't far from here.
A walk will clear my head,
but it won't do much for my stomach.
Bloody heck, the footpath is really uneven.
Maybe it's something to do with the mine?
All that digging underground.
The old man reckons the whole town will collapse
and disappear into a giant pit.
I wish *he'd* disappear into a giant pit!

Here's Colleen's place.
Up and tumble over the fence
into the bushes beside her room.
How did my clothes get so dirty?
I'm just sitting here,
innocent, I swear,
giving my eyes time to focus …
through her window.
And there she is,
getting out of bed,
wearing just a nightie,
a very short nightie,

as she heads out to the dunny
in the backyard.

My eyes follow her,
but I don't move.
I can't move.
When she walks back up the path
I see her ankles,
fine slim ankles,
and I gulp so hard
I'm sure she can hear me.
But she doesn't look around.
She hurries inside,
and I watch as she snuggles down into bed.
Then I stagger away from the bushes,
thinking a thousand things at once,
feeling mad sober
and wild drunk
all at the same time.

Albert Holding

My wife and I don't talk much.
Not since I got home from up north
and she asked me questions,
too many questions,
about what I'd done,
what I'd seen,
what I planned to do
now that the family was back together.
It only took a few hours
for her to mention the mine
and the jobs begging to be filled
and how some boys
were leaving school
to work down the pits
because the money's so good,
and everyone in town
is buying one of them new fridges,
and how the Bennetts have moved
into a bigger house
now there's two breadwinners.
That's when I slammed the chair back
and leaned over the table,
pointing toward town.
"I'm never going down that bloody mine again!
And neither are the boys.
They either leave town,
if they got half a brain,

or they find whatever work they can
above ground, in the sunshine."
She doesn't understand.
No one can,
unless they've been down the pits
where men get buried
and all the management does
is put a cairn at the entrance
to remind us of their sacrifice.
Each miner touches the inscription
"for luck"
before disappearing.
Not me.
Not my boys.

My wife and I,
we don't talk much.

Mr. Butcher

In the city, the streets reek
of perfume, beer, and smoke.
It's easy to find what I want,
no matter how late it is.
She has hazel eyes
and glistening black hair.
We go to the Royal Hotel,
offering rooms by the hour,
and climb the creaking stairs
with stained carpet.
The odor of fried food
blows through an open window.
She switches on a lamp,
which throws a pale light
over the unmade bed.
When she asks my name
I answer, "Eddie. Eddie Holding."
That insolent kid wouldn't know what to do.
Her perfume is so strong my eyes water.
I tell her what I want.
My hand reaches for her hair,
a slick of fine weave,
her thick lipstick on my cheek
and the touch of her cool skin …
and suddenly I think of the classroom,
my weekday world,
so I lean heavily on her soft body.

I'm so thrilled and so ashamed
all at the same time.
I push harder,
trying to forget everything,
but I see the blankness in her eyes
and that's when I ram
as rough as I dare.
I want to drive that emptiness away
until it's replaced by fear.
With one last lunge
I groan like an animal,
roll off, and keep my eyes closed
for as long as possible,
even when I hear her dressing.
"Time's up, Eddie."
She's standing there
looking older than she did an hour ago,
with her hair a charcoal mess
and clothes slouched on.
She stuffs the money in her handbag,
says good-bye, and walks out,
leaving the door open
to remind me this room
is rented by the hour,
not the night.

Eddie

Larry stinks of beer
and mumbles to himself
as he climbs into bed
on the other side of our small room.
He's gonna snore all night
and in the morning
roll over with a headache and a temper.
He'll stumble outside
and throw up under the lemon tree.

I've got no chores tomorrow
so I jump out of bed,
climb over my rank brother,
and step out the open window.
I wrap the blanket tight around me
and follow the track up into the hills.
The path is overgrown
with swaying grass stalks and banksia.
I lie in the cool grass under the rosewood tree
and look up at the looming cliff.
It has the face of an old man
with one eye closed
and a scar on his chin,
a coal-seam scar
too high to mine.
I close my eyes,
listening to the rustle of the leaves

and the distant siren from the mine.
The afternoon shift finishing at midnight.
I sleep beside the Coal Man
battered into the cliff,
miles above my town.

Mr. Butcher

The valley is covered in mist
as I return on the mail train.
Back to my flat
to boil the kettle
and sit by the window
with my feet on the ledge,
drinking my tea,
thinking of her shoulders,
the arch of her back,
her thick black hair.
And although I try to stop myself,
I'm already imagining next weekend.
This time a blonde,
with a ponytail,
a long ponytail.
A young lady.
Someone who doesn't put on lipstick
quite so thick,
who doesn't drench herself in cheap perfume
that rankles through my clothes
so I'm afraid everyone in town can smell it.
I leave the clothes to soak
in the washtub downstairs.
Next week I want someone fresh,
with alabaster skin.

Monday morning,
I pack my briefcase
with this week's homework
and try to steady my thoughts.
The students are walking to school.
In all the time I've lived here,
in this wretched flat,
not one person has ever looked up
to wave hello.

THREE

Town and City

Albert Holding

Every morning before dawn
I stumble out of bed
in the chill damp of our house
to make my lunch for the day ahead.
Yesterday's bread wrapped in wax paper
and a thermos of sweet black tea.
The boys are still asleep,
fidgeting in their hand-built beds.
My wife has a whisper of gray hair on her temple.
Her dressing gown tossed across the blanket.
On our bedside table are two photos.
One of our wedding day.
All I remember is slicking my hair down
with Brylcreem
and the little tail that wouldn't sit
at the nape of my neck.
My hair was laughing at me behind my back.
I'm in uniform in the other photo,
the hat tilted just right.
I'm grinning like someone
who doesn't know what's about to happen.
The smile of a fool;
a happy idiot.
One day I'll take that photo
and toss it in the wood stove.
Replace it with one of the boys.
As I close the front door,

the click of the lock
sounds like loading a gun.
My heavy boots crack the frost.
The sky is charcoal gray.
Nobody wakes to see me off now.
Pretty girls kissed me on victory day,
their lips soft red petals brushing my face.
Now I'm just a married man in farm overalls.
I remember my arms tight around their waists,
closing my eyes to their rich inviting smell.
It stayed on my uniform for days,
until the wife washed and stored it
in the wardrobe to be eaten by moths.
Victory lasted precisely one day.
Now I work like a mule
alone in a mud-bog paddock
and the only enemy left is myself.

Mr. Carter

Pete Grainger is a smart lad,
and I guess there are worse places
to be stationed than your hometown.
So I wrote it up in the paper
with a big splash.
"Local Policeman Returns to Help His Community."
Pete does his best.
He wants to see the town prosper,
so he goes easy on Mr. Wright
when he gets drunk.
Pete escorts him home,
never to the lockup,
because you can't have the mine manager in jail,
now can you?
And Mr. Calder never heard about his son
stealing the milk money after dusk.
Pete gave the kid a good talking-to
and a solid kick where the bruise won't show.
No one knows,
no one was told,
but I'm a newspaperman
who can smell which way the wind blows.
I'm not broadcasting the town troubles
for all the world to read.
Pete's job would send me balmy.
Filling out forms,
patrolling the town,

waiting for something to happen.

And all the time wishing for a little excitement,

then, when it comes,

shuddering

because it means someone is up to no good.

Pete's the poor beggar

who has to deal with it.

It's true to say

that nobody welcomes a copper

knocking on their door

in the small hours of the night.

Sergeant Grainger

I patrol the evening streets
in fading light,
nodding to each of the store owners
as they shut up shop,
asking if there's anything I can do.
Mrs. Kain grabs my hand and pleads,
"Yes, Sergeant, more customers, please!"
She's joking, but I wish I could help.
For all that Kenneth Paley says about a new town
with a better life and brighter future,
it's still the same sleepy place it always was.
Except Fridays,
when there's always a brawl at the pub,
with two blokes squaring off outside
and a crowd gathered,
laying bets,
shouting and cheering.
In an hour I'll have to drive the loser home,
hoping he doesn't bleed on the upholstery.
He'll try to remind me
when we were both just kids in town,
riding bikes and kicking footballs.
He'll tell me I should have joined him
down the mine, at a real job.
Just like our fathers, years ago,
when they were alive.
I'll spend Saturday cleaning up the mess

and Sunday in church, watching the men
praying silently for forgiveness
or a win in the lottery.
I'm not what you'd call religious, especially.
But it goes with the job.
Be seen.
Blend in.

Colleen

Mr. Butcher wrote at the bottom of my essay,
"A work of talent and promise.
Beautiful."
When I glanced up
he was smiling at me.
His eyes dropped a fraction
and he cleared his throat,
quickly turning to the blackboard.
In the far corner, someone groaned.
Mr. Butcher spun around
and threw a piece of chalk at Eddie,
who ducked as it bounced off the wall
and shattered into pieces.
Eddie leaned over and picked it all up,
placing each piece in a neat pile on his desk.
No one said a word.
We all looked down at the floor.
Mr. Butcher walked slowly around the class
until he stood behind my chair.
I crossed my legs nervously
and sat up as straight as I could manage,
wondering what he was going to say.
"Colleen. Would you do us the honor
of reading your work this morning?"
He touched my shoulder
and pulled back my chair.
I had no choice but to stand

and walk to the front of the class,
my fingers gripping the paper tightly
with the thought of all those eyes watching me.
Mr. Butcher sat at my chair
and pointed accusingly at Eddie.
"We'll have absolute quiet, Holding.
You may learn something more valuable
than how to avoid flying objects."
Most of the class giggled,
except Larry, who leaned forward and winked.
My voice read the words,
while the rest of me wished
I was back in my chair
and the likes of Larry and Butcher
would just leave me alone.

Sally

I've started praying
because
ever since Eddie and me kissed
on the riverbank
I've been having thoughts
that I'm not sure I should be,
and maybe I'm cursed
or blessed
with the best imagination a girl can have
because what I see in my mind
makes me feel all warm inside,
too warm,
and I don't know what to do with it.
So I kneel by the bed
and talk to God
about what I'm thinking,
and I keep my eyes closed
but that only makes my mind work faster.
I try to see Saint Catherine
in her long dark robes,
but all I end up with is Eddie and me
in a bed together
under soft white sheets
with nothing on,
naked,
and he's cuddling me,
kissing me,

and my hands start to wander.
I feel things
I've never felt before
and it's too much.

I'm alone here,
thinking of Eddie
and tingling.
I'm sure God is watching,
calling out my name,
calling me back,
but I can only hear
the rush of my breath
and the touch of skin on skin.

This isn't supposed to happen.
Is it?

Sergeant Grainger

When I left the police academy,
uniform pressed and clean,
buttons shiny,
notepad and pencil in top pocket,
I never thought I'd end up back here.
A sergeant.
That's my title.
They gave me that
because only a sergeant
can run a police station alone,
and there was no way
they'd send two officers out here
where nothing much happens
but drunk and disorderly,
and the odd teenager pinching stuff
off the loading dock at the back of Paley's,
or an ice block from Sunset Café.
Three years' training
for booting kids up the bum,
filling out forms,
and keeping an eye on Barney Haggerty,
making sure he doesn't sleep out in the park
once too often.
Old Barney is so full of metho,
I'm careful not to light a match too close
in case we both go up in flames.
I used to like a beer or three.

But a copper at the bar
wouldn't have any authority,
not in this town.
So I stock up on lager
and put my feet on the lounge at home,
open a bottle,
and think a wife wouldn't go astray.
But finding someone out here,
there's two chances—
none and Buckley's.

Colleen

Ruth, Wendy, and me
skip down Main Street
for a celebration milkshake at Sunset Café.
Our netball team won!
Now we're in the finals.
Mrs. Kain says we already look like champions
and adds extra malt.
It tastes creamy and sweet.
Mrs. Kain stands beside our table
waiting to top up our glasses.
Mr. Butcher comes in,
tips his hat, and smiles at us.
Ruth says,
"You going to come to the final, sir?
Next weekend?"
He holds up his overnight bag and shrugs.
Off to the city again.
I wish he'd stay there!
Wendy wants to go home past the pub
and meet some of the older boys.
"Let's really celebrate."
She leans in close.
"With something stronger than a vanilla malted."
We giggle at the thought of the young miners
slipping beers out the side window
and offering to walk us home the long way.
I'm tempted.

Les Johnston will be there.

When we leave,

Mr. Butcher offers to pay for our milkshakes.

He passes the money to Mrs. Kain,

brushes my arm, and says,

"Congratulations, girls.

A fine achievement."

His breath smells of mouthwash,

and he's got far too much grease in his hair.

On the footpath,

Wendy loosens her blouse,

smooths her skirt,

and says,

"We might find someone tall and handsome.

And sober."

We link arms and walk toward the pub.

Larry

Sometimes a bloke gets lucky.
Wendy and Ruth
and the lovely Colleen
look to be up for a bit of fun.
I step from the doorway of the hardware
and ask them if they want a drink,
just to be friendly, you know.
Wendy asks where I got it from.
"I've got my own supply.
I'll show you, if you want."
I offer Wendy the bottle,
but Ruth says no
and pulls her arm away.
"Go on, have some," I say.
I move toward them
and trip on the cracked footpath.
To stop myself from falling
I reach out and grab Wendy's shoulders,
and she screams.
"Settle down, settle down.
I just fell, that's all."
Ruth sticks up her nose
and says,
"You're drunk,"
which is bloody obvious
and I say so,
but that doesn't go down too well,

and they turn to leave.

Smart-arse Ruth says,

"You pong like an old man."

Looking at Colleen, I say,

"But I do everything else like a young man."

Ruth pulls Colleen and Wendy away.

I shout after them,

"I'll be behind the pub, if you're interested."

Colleen might follow,

if she can shake those two tight sheilas.

Albert Holding

Fatty Paley does his Friday pub trick,
offering everyone a drink
and making a show
of slapping us all on the back
or shaking hands
and asking if there's anything he can do.
Yeah, piss off, Fatty,
that's what I want to say,
but, hell,
it's a free beer,
so I drink it down.
Fatty sounds a little sozzled himself,
wandering from table to table,
swaying as he offers his clammy hand,
talking louder than he should.
He's a dimwit of the highest order.
Before closing, I order two beers
and walk outside to smoke in peace.
Those three young sheilas
look to be having fun.
I wouldn't mind that sort of company.
One of them is drinking a beer,
passed through the back window.
They're laughing and talking
to the young blokes inside.
The blonde one looks in my direction
and quickly hides the glass.

I shout,

"Don't worry, love.

I'm not dobbing on anyone."

If Fatty sees them

he'll try to buy their vote.

He'd be too slow to notice they're too young.

Too young for voting, anyway.

Mayor Paley

My wife Wilma
doesn't understand.
She accuses me,
yes, *accuses* me
of going to the pub for the beer.
"It's work," I say.
I'm the mayor.
I should be available,
ready to listen to anyone who complains
or needs help.
Like the time I offered a tent to the Holdings
until they built that ramshackle heap
they call a home, way out beside the river.
They didn't have a roof over their heads,
not without my generous offer.
The pub is where I meet people;
where anybody, no matter who they are,
can come up and shake the mayor's hand.
Wilma spends the evening
knitting in the front room—
another oversized bloody cardigan—
waiting for me to come home.
My tea,
cold on the table.
To hell with that.
I'm having another beer.
I'm working.

Larry

Look at those girls
hanging around the pub,
accepting beers off the Johnston boys.
I pick up a rock,
round and smooth,
and walk past Blind O'Brien's.
The lights are out, as usual.
He can't use them anyway.
I chuck the rock,
and it explodes on the roof,
like a hand grenade.
The bloody grass is slippery with dew,
and I land flat on my bum,
laughing at the thought of O'Brien
hiding in his bed.
I'm having trouble getting up,
feeling a bit giddy
and careful not to spill my beer,
when some coward whacks me from behind,
hard across my legs.
It's O'Brien waving his cane,
and one blow glances off my shoulder.
The stupid old man finds his range
and hits me again and again
until I push past him,
running down the street,
calling out,

"You blind bastard!"
I stumble away,
watching him lean on his cane, smiling.
He can wait out there all night,
I don't care.
I'll pay him back
some other time.

Mr. Carter

There goes Frank O'Connor's daughter,
Colleen, walking past with her head bowed,
as if she's eager to get somewhere.
The raucous sound of voices
echoes from the pub,
and the occasional crash of glass
shatters Main Street.
I make a habit of only two beers, early,
well before closing,
and then I return to do the accounts for the week.
Since my wife died
I prefer to spend my evenings
working in the front room of my office.
If I stay too long at the pub
with the miners offering the shout
and suggesting stories for the front page,
I get maudlin and start thinking of Grace.
It's been four years since she passed.
We couldn't have children,
and in a marriage of thirty-two years
I guess that's my only regret.
There's a divine plan there somewhere,
of that I believe,
only sometimes, late at night,
I can't see why He'd take Grace
and leave me with my writings,
my books and figures,

and a knot deep in my stomach.
I've tried praying.
It gives me comfort.
But not as much as a cup of tea
and a ginger nut biscuit.

Eddie

I'm waiting for Butcher to show.
He's late.
Tonight I'm ready with my good jacket
and enough money to follow him,
to find out what he gets up to away from here.
He probably has relatives
in the posh part of the city,
with a painted fence
and a cobblestone path.
I hear the train whistle
and the sound of hurrying footsteps.
He runs like a girl,
swinging his arms low,
his bag banging on his knees.
I climb down from the tree,
skirting around the far side of the station.
I'm sure I can make the last carriage
after Butcher gets in the front one.
The train approaches,
its rushing rhythm beats hard like my heart.
Butcher drops his bag on the platform
and bends over double,
clutching his stomach,
breathing deeply and coughing.
Don't have a heart attack, Butcher.
As he opens the door,
I scamper out from the bushes

and jump in the back carriage.
I stay low in the seat until I hear the whistle,
and we move slowly away from Burruga.
The train starts the long rise
out of the valley
as I look around the compartment.
We climb Jaspers Hill
and I realize what I've done.
I'm heading to the city,
and there's no train home
until morning.

Eddie

I feel like laughing,
laughing out loud.
I've never been alone to the city before,
and here I am on a train
with enough money for the return fare,
maybe a pie,
but certainly not enough for a hotel room.
Maybe I'll ask Mr. Butcher
if I can sleep in the shed.
There's no one else in the carriage.
No one to tell Dad.
He'd kill me if he found out.
I drop the window and lean out,
letting the air cool my sweat.
In the half-light I can make out the shapes of horses,
slender and quiet in the paddocks
as the train labors up the hill.
At least I won't have to hear Larry snoring tonight
and then smell our bedroom
when he wakes in his own vomit.
This is an adventure.

Eddie

I'm jostled by the crowds at Central Station,
all looking like they're going somewhere important,
while I loiter behind Mr. Butcher
as he walks briskly through the sandstone exit.
He heads up a long, wide avenue
with bright lights on the hill,
lots of flashing neon signs
and pubs on every corner.
I can't believe there are this many people in the city.
It's like Friday night in Burruga
a hundred times over.
Mr. Butcher will never see me,
even if he bothers to look.
This doesn't seem like a place people live.
There are shops and tattoo joints
and gloomy parks
where I hear voices and laughter.
Someone's having a party outdoors.
Mr. Butcher walks slower
and he stops occasionally,
looking in shop windows
in a distracted sort of way.
I don't think he's heading home at all.
A young lady with long flame-red hair
comes up behind him
and they start talking,
but they're not smiling or anything,

like they know each other.
It's not like that at all.
The lady twirls and walks toward me,
and I keep my eyes down.
She walks up to me
and says something I don't hear properly.
So I say, "Pardon?"
She squeezes my arm and says,
"Aren't you a polite one.
How about it, sonny?"
How about what?
Then I smell her perfume
and notice the cut of her dress,
and I try not to look at her breasts
in case she thinks I'm rude
but it's kind of hard not to look.
"How about it?"
She's offering something
ladies don't really offer,
well, not in Burruga.
I don't know what to say,
and I see Mr. Butcher
a long way up the road
about to turn the corner,
so I quickly shake my head
and I rush after him
with a thousand thoughts
churning through my brain.

Eddie

Now Mr. Butcher is talking to someone
who looks as young as me,
with long, shiny blonde hair,
and she's wearing a tight dress
and high heels,
ready for a date.
She walks beside Mr. Butcher
and lights a cigarette.
She leads him into a block of flats on the corner.
The door slams behind them.
I creep around the side
and climb the paling fence,
jump down behind some bushes,
and feel my way to the back,
afraid there might be a dog.
There's a light on in the back room,
so I sneak toward the shed.
I hear their voices
as she moves to the window,
pulls back the curtain,
and flicks her cigarette into the yard.
She's naked!
I can see her breasts
and forget all about Mr. Butcher
until his shadow moves behind
and pulls her toward him.
She quickly moves away,

walks to the door,

and switches off the light.

I could go closer now,

if I wanted,

but I'm still trying to take it all in.

He's in there with a girl half his age,

and I'm wandering around the backyard

with no idea what to do.

Mr. Butcher

Blonde hair framing her face
my fingers all over her body
her enticing aroma
her languid eyes
her arm flung back
blonde hair
her fingers in small fists
my weight pressing
her body like soft talc
blonde hair
I can't get enough blonde hair.

Eddie

Mr. Butcher and the girl
are inside for twenty minutes,
and the sounds I hear tell me
they're not just talking.
She's can't be his girlfriend.
She's not much older than Sally.
So why is she doing it?
The light flicks on in the room
and in my brain.
For money!
I laugh at how dim I am.
Why would anyone do that with hopeless Butcher
if not for money.
The first question that springs to mind is,
how much?
It would need to be a bloody lot of moolah.
The door slams
and I see the girl at the window
still naked,
smoking a cigarette,
looking out at the yard.
I'm sure Butcher has left,
but I can't follow him.
The girl is watching.
I remain still and hidden.
I don't care where Butcher goes now.

Sergeant Grainger

The phone rings
and I expect it's Johnno, the publican
calling me about this week's fight
between two drunk miners
and a disagreement over
whose bloody shout it is.
They're wasting good drinking time,
if you ask me.
But it's Mrs. O'Connor,
wondering where her daughter is.
Frank will be back from the pub soon
and angry as hell if Colleen's not home.
I know Colleen.
Smart and pretty
and not the type to get up to mischief.
So I promise Mrs. O'Connor
I'll check out the netball courts
and Main Street,
and I wonder aloud
if she isn't visiting a girlfriend
to celebrate their win.
That seems to settle her nerves.
She gives me the names
of the other players on the team,
and I tell her I'll door-knock
for the next hour
and drop by soon with Colleen.

I pull on my overcoat,
my sergeant's hat,
and head to the car.
Well, at least it's not an all-in brawl.

Sergeant Grainger

The first families I visit
are sitting down to late supper.
One by one, husbands come to the door,
all of them swaying slightly,
holding a bottle and inviting me in.
Everyone's a friend when you're sloshed.
Most are too drunk to understand my questions.
They slap me on the back
and say obvious things like,
"Yeah. Colleen. I know her.
She's Frank and Betty's daughter."
And they fumble through their pockets
looking for smokes or a pipe.
Wendy Sutton says they had a milkshake together
and came straight home,
leaving Colleen outside the café.
As I close the front gate
I realize that doesn't make sense.
If they were going home,
they'd walk up Main Street together,
before separating.
Wendy mentioned Ruth Weaver.
The Weavers live two blocks away,
and I walk with a creeping sense
that someone is telling tales.
Mrs. Weaver answers the door.
George is asleep, she says.

He's had so much to drink
nothing is waking him until morning.
She lets me speak to Ruth in the sitting room.
The young lady fidgets with her necklace
and keeps glancing toward the kitchen,
hoping her mum can't hear.
"The three of us went to the pub.
We just stood outside,
talking, that's all.
Someone gave Colleen a shandy
and we all took a sip. Just one sip."
Ruth leans forward and whispers,
"Colleen left before us.
Wendy and me wanted to stay.
We weren't drunk.
Not like Larry Holding.
He was so wonky he almost knocked Wendy over."
Mrs. Weaver comes into the room
with her arms folded tightly across her chest.
She's heard every word.
I say, "Thank you, Ruth.
For your honesty."
It won't help her
when George wakes, hung over,
and gets an earful over breakfast from the wife
about his daughter, drinking,
and taking after him.

Sergeant Grainger

Albert Holding closes the door
and steps out into the yard.
He walks a distance from the house
before speaking.
"So why are you asking me?
There's lots of houses
between here and the pub.
Have you knocked on them all?"
He stands with his hands on his hips,
in challenge.
"A friend of Colleen said your Larry—"
"My Larry what?"
"Larry was drinking.
And he offered them some."
Albert Holding turns away and swears.
He walks a few steps toward the house,
then says,
"Listen. I saw them girls outside the pub.
Okay?
Drinking with some young blokes.
My Larry wasn't one of them."
He shakes his head in anger.
"If you want to find out what happened,
piss off back to town
and ask some people who do know.
Leave my boy alone.
He'll be in enough trouble

when he wakes up tomorrow."

Albert's as mad as a cut snake,

but right now, I couldn't care less.

"Mr. Holding.

A girl is missing.

If that means asking you about your son,

then so be it."

Albert looks like he wants to punch someone.

"Do your bloody job, Grainger.

Find the girl."

He walks back inside,

slamming the door so hard

the windows rattle fit to break.

As I return to the car,

I'm shaking with anger.

Where is Colleen?

And who is she with?

Larry

I'm glad Eddie isn't home.
I couldn't stand him looking at me,
asking where I've been
and how much I've drunk.
I just want to sleep
and be left alone to forget.
I kick the blanket off
and feel the beer rumbling deep in my stomach.
That bloody Ruth Weaver is a stuck-up bitch,
looking down her nose at me.
Just 'cause I stumbled.
Those girls spent the night
flirting with the blokes from the mine.
I saw them, from behind the water tank.
It made my blood boil
when Les Johnston offered a shandy to Colleen
and she drank it down, giggling.
Take a drink with him,
but not from me.
All those mornings in the library wasted.
I rush to the door
and make the backyard
before I throw up.
The cool breeze dries the sweat on my forehead
as I squat in the yard
and heave my guts up.

Eddie

I step out into the light,
ready for her scream,
ready to run.
She just lights another cigarette
and looks at me,
daring me to do something.
I step closer
so I can see her eyes
and she can see mine.
"That bloke,
he's my teacher."
As if she cares.
She keeps looking at me
with her sharp green eyes,
and I try to hold their stare
or else I'll look where I shouldn't
and she'll see me looking.
She makes a scoffing sound
and casually flicks the cigarette into the yard.
"Well, for a teacher,
he doesn't know much."
Then she smiles at her own little joke.
I smile, too,
glad Butcher is miles away
while I'm standing here in someone's yard
looking at a naked girl
who's looking back at me

and asking,

with a faint smirk

as she beckons me with her fingers,

"What's your name?"

Eddie

She says,
"Well, Eddie.
I've got all night.
If you can afford it."
I gulp,
even though it's the funniest thing
I've ever heard.
I reach deep into my pocket,
take out the coins,
and hold them up into the light.
"That's all I've got.
Enough for a pie
and the train home.
But thanks for asking."
I'm not trying to be rude or anything.
She stares over my head for a long time
until I feel nervous standing here alone,
not saying a word,
not knowing where to look.
Then she glances down at me
and says,
"I was as polite and nice as you.
Until I came here.
Maybe I've got time for charity,
if you're interested."
My hands start shaking.
Larry and all the blokes in town

would jump at the chance to do it with a city girl.

"I … I … have a girlfriend.

At home."

A dog barks from next door

as she leans forward and says,

"Don't end up like your teacher, kid.

He's a loser."

She draws the curtains

and is gone.

Sergeant Grainger

Mrs. O'Connor stands on the top step.

Her husband waits at the front gate.

"She's not home, Pete.

If I catch the bloke she's with, let me tell you,

he'll be getting more than a clip around the ear.

And I don't expect trouble from you over it."

Frank did it tough in the war.

It's more than my job's worth to argue the toss.

Frank removes his hat

and wipes his forehead with the back of his hand.

"The wife is beside herself, Pete.

I'll stay with her for a while.

Find the pair of them

and bring Colleen home, quick smart, will you?"

I nod in answer,

relieved he hasn't asked to come with me.

People in town don't say no to Frank.

"I'll be back within the hour."

Sergeant Grainger

If Colleen is with somebody,
they'll be at Taylors Bend.
There's a standing joke
that half the kids in school
were conceived down there.
The soft sand and grassy bank
make a perfect lovers' lane.
If I catch the ratbags at it,
I'll give them both a tongue-lashing
for keeping me out all night
and putting up with the likes of Holding.
I whistle as I walk down the track
and flash the torch beam well ahead.
Give them time to get decent.

The light passes over a shape
on the sand by the water's edge.
Bloody hell.
It's Colleen!
One arm dangling in the river,
one arm on her chest.
There's blood on her face.
Jesus! No!
I rush to her side
and touch her cold skin,
hoping against hope for a pulse.

The girl is dead.

I reel into the bushes to vomit
until nothing comes but bile and tears.
I sink to my hands and knees
to catch my breath,
my eyes tightly shut,
and a pain throbbing against my temple.
Behind me lies a girl
admired by everybody in town.
Frank and Betty's daughter.
Sweat prickles on my forehead,
and I shiver with the breeze across the water,
across Colleen.

I return to her body
and start searching for evidence, anything,
before I tell the town what's happened.
Once I do that
this place will be a swarm of anger,
kicking up sand,
masking clues that must still be here.
Every second I look
Colleen's body lies there
and pleads for covering.
Her body begs to be taken away
and put into a warm bed
with the sheets pulled high,
even though nothing can help now.

I can't stay here much longer.

Colleen deserves better than this.

Her skirt is torn and twisted around her hips,

a smear of dark sand on the fabric.

Scuffed footprints, shattered glass,

and a cigarette butt

that could have been here for days

or minutes …

Who in my town could do this?

FOUR

Cold Skin

Eddie

I wander back to Central Station
and bunk down in the huge waiting room.
Moths fly around the light
as I roll my jumper into a pillow
and lie down,
hoping no one will disturb me
before the train home tomorrow.
A kerosene heater burns in the corner,
and I hope it lasts all night.

Now I know why Mr. Butcher
comes here every weekend.
But I can't tell anyone.
No one would believe me.

Butcher can't get a wife
so he pays for it.
He's not the first to do that.
So why am I following him,
like some Peeping Tom?
Maybe I'll let Mr. Butcher know what I've seen.
What then?
Better marks in exams?
The bastard would deny it
and make up some story.
If Dad found out,
I'd be in deep trouble.

As I drift between sleep and the city,
I picture Sally and Colleen
and how Mr. Butcher always smiles at them.
I thought it was because they got good grades.
He likes young girls.
The creep likes young girls.

Sergeant Grainger

As I drive back to town,
I can't bear the thought of leaving her there.
Someone else finding her.
And late evening dew
settling on her body.
I knock on the front door of the *Guardian* office.
Mr. Carter will phone the undertaker
and do what has to be done,
without question.
It's ironic,
the town newspaperman
is the only person I can trust
to keep it quiet for tonight.

The tremor in my voice
tells him something is terribly wrong.
I blurt out my story,
and he doesn't say a word.
He crosses himself and asks,
"Do you want me to come with you, Pete?
To tell Frank and Betty?"
I shake my head.
"No. It's my duty, Mr. Carter."
And a bastard of a job at that.
We shake hands for no particular reason
and arrange to meet back at the river
with Mr. Smyth, the undertaker,
in fifteen minutes,
to bring Colleen back to town.

Sergeant Grainger

There's a cricket on my windscreen
when I park outside the O'Connors'.
He crawls along the glass
and hops onto the warm bonnet,
rubbing his wings for all it's worth.
When I was a kid,
we'd put them in a glass jar
with a few pinholes in the lid
and hide them in our parents' room.
Dad would rampage around half the night,
shouting, swearing,
pulling the sheets off the bed,
tossing stuff out of the wardrobe.
In the next room,
my sister and me
did our best not to scream with laughter.
My sister lives in the city now,
with a daughter of her own.
The last time I visited,
we sat in her back garden,
the crickets kicking up a racket,
watching her little girl
playing in the sandpit.
"It's the greatest gift, Pete.
A child."

Every light in the O'Connor house is on.

Mr. Carter

Pete takes the camera from my hands.
I can't bring myself to photograph the girl
even though it must be done.
The flash blazes in the cold air,
lighting everything in a vicious glow.
The Bible says:
"Walk by faith, not by sight."
We drape a sheet over Colleen
and carry her gently
to the undertaker's van.
Mr. Smyth drives away as we return to the river.
I splash cold water on my face.
To be honest
I don't want to leave this place.
Let me go back to yesterday
when this town was full
of miners and shopkeepers,
clerks and accountants,
schoolchildren and farmers,
husbands and wives,
sons and daughters.

From tomorrow,
until Pete finds out who did this,
our town will be full of murderers.

Eddie

The journey home is sleepy
as the train stops at every station,
even though no one gets on or off.
I think of the girl last night,
naked.
Only I imagine her as Sally,
and she lets me into the room …
I put my arms around her
and touch her soft skin.
Sally moves her hand along her bare stomach,
and I get goose bumps,
crossing my legs quickly
at the thought of what we could do
together in the city, all night to spare.
The train whistle scares me awake,
and I smell the coal smoke
as we round the final bend into town.
A chill breeze blows through the carriage.
I make a promise to myself
to watch Butcher,
not to let him near Sally.
That's a good enough excuse
for being with her.
As the train winds down the mountain
I look out at Burruga.
It seems so much smaller from up here.
The river meanders to the east,

the houses all crowd along the cross streets,
except our place, of course.
The sports oval is covered in early morning mist,
and the mine rises above everything.
That's the only reason there's a town
in this tight little valley.

Mr. Carter

No chance of sleep last night.
I just sat in my chair,
watching the street outside,
thinking,
I was one of the last to see the poor child.
I cursed myself,
getting up for a cup of tea
after she walked by.
Someone may have followed.
But why would I have acted?
An old man finds regret
wherever he looks.
Before dawn
a stray dog walked across the road,
sniffing for food
or company.
He wandered to the window,
saw me watching,
wagged his tail,
barked once,
and trotted away.

As the sun beams in,
I draw the blinds to shut out the town.
Today I'll draft an obituary for Monday's edition.
What I write won't be good enough.
It won't ease the pain for anyone.

But I must say something
to make us proud for having known Colleen.
For her parents.
For all of us.

Eddie

I climb through the window
real quietly.
Larry is snoring, as usual.
Mum and Dad are in the kitchen
talking in urgent whispers.
They haven't noticed the kettle
boiling on the stove.
I must be in trouble.
They don't say much to each other,
not since Dad came home.
I fill the bathroom sink
and dunk my head,
scrubbing the city away.
In the mirror
a face rough as guts stares back,
but I can't sleep.
Time for some cock-and-bull story
they won't believe,
no matter what I say.

Dad looks away when I enter.
He coughs and shuffles in his chair.
He seems embarrassed.
Mum asks if I want eggs,
wiping her hands on her apron.
They don't even know I've been gone.
Larry's got up to no good, I reckon.

Dad walks outside to get more firewood,
and Mum fusses at the stove,
her shoulders stiff
as she waits for the pan to heat up.
As soon as I finish my eggs
I'm getting out of here,
before Larry wakes
and the shouting starts.

Eddie

Sally's Spot is at the bottom of her street.
In the shade under our rope tree
there's a patch of grass soft enough for sleeping.
All I hear is the flow of the stream
and the distant cackle of cockatoos.
When I left this morning,
the strap was missing from the hook
behind the door.
One day, Larry will strike back at Dad
and there'll be hell to pay.

Before I drift off
there's a noise from the bushes.
Sally runs down the track
and jumps into my arms,
her head tight against my chest.
I don't know what to say,
so I hold her close.
She's crying,
hiding her face in my shirt.
Has Butcher done something already?
But he wouldn't be back from town yet.
She grips my arms and looks up at me.
"Isn't it terrible?"
She sees I don't understand
and starts crying again.
"What?"

She sits down in the grass.
Her lip starts to quiver,
her hands shake.
"Colleen is dead!
Mum told me this morning,
when I woke."
Tears squeeze down her face.
"Mum said she was murdered."

I close my eyes
and gently wrap my arms around Sally.
All I can think of is Butcher
running late for the train.

Sally

I fold against Eddie's chest,
my eyes stinging with tears.
I'm torn between staying beside the river
or taking his hand and leaving town,
just leaving, somehow,
never coming back.
I want to escape this place
and what's happened,
what's going to happen.
That's what scares me most.
What now?
Who do we trust?
Eddie strokes my hair,
and I know it's him and me and family.
No one else.
I shiver at the creeping thought
of someone living here among us,
doing what he did to poor Colleen.
Talking to each of us in the daylight
and wandering dangerous at night ...

Mr. Carter

I pass the bare rosebushes,
stark in the front garden,
and knock quietly at the door.
Mrs. O'Connor's face is pale and tear-stained.
Overnight her body has shrunk.
She shuffles into the lounge room
with the curtains partly drawn
and the photos of Colleen
on the mantel above the fireplace.
She says,
"You'll have tea, won't you?"
Then she stands looking
at some children walking past,
carrying fishing lines.
One boy is tossing his hat in the air
and trying to catch it behind his back.
As they pass, her hollow eyes follow them
all the way down the street.
I sit opposite Mr. O'Connor
and offer him my apologies and the obituary.
"I won't print anything without your word, Frank."
His lips tighten as he reads the page,
the paper white against his brown calloused hands.
I'm sorry to do this
to a man who's been through enough
these past few years.
He hands the page to his wife

and looks across the room to Colleen's picture,
listening to her absence,
breathing deeply the air she can't share.
He sits up straight
and looks at me for what seems like ages,
then he leans forward and offers his hand.
"Thanks, Mr. Carter.
Thanks for your kind thoughts."
Men walk through tragedy, quietly,
calm and precise on the outside,
tearing themselves to shreds inside.

Sergeant Grainger

Today I start asking questions
and losing friends.
Everyone pushed for details of last night
will get nervous and call in our history.
I'll spend the day being reminded
of long-ago drinking sessions
before I left for the academy
and hard yards on the footy field
when we had a losing streak
that lasted for years.
No one will want to talk about here and now.
Not to a copper investigating a murder.

But I figure it's just like the schoolyard,
you know,
when someone broke a window
or got into a fight.
You could tell who was guilty,
who was lying,
by looking into their eyes.
That's what I'm doing all this week.
Looking deep into my hometown
and studying the reflection.
Mayor Paley phones me early
and suggests a reward.
He calls it "an incentive."
I waste valuable time

explaining that it isn't how things work.

He keeps repeating

"No stone left unturned."

As if it's all so easy.

Like getting elected mayor

when no one else wants the job.

Sergeant Grainger

The Johnston twins don't say much.
They saw Larry Holding
hanging around behind the pub
and admit drinking their fair share.
For two years they've been going down the mine
and have faced worse things
than a suspicious policeman.
They keep calling me *mate*
to remind me of my place.
Les says,
"I passed her a shandy and she took a drink.
That's all.
She's too young anyway."
Then he realizes how that sounds.
"Sorry. I didn't mean nothing.
She's Frank's daughter, for pity's sake.
No one in their right mind would touch her."
Barry says,
"Look. She left before the other two girls.
That's all we know.
Ask them. They'll tell you."
They're both dressed in overalls
preparing for the next shift.
Les glances at his watch and reaches for his bag.
"Do us a favor, mate.
Don't mention the shandy to Frank."

Mr. Butcher

Hard-working men like me
should be left in peace
on a Sunday afternoon.
I've only just walked in from the train.
Sergeant Grainger is too interested
in what time I left on Friday night.
He should mind his own business,
but something in his manner
tells me not to provoke him.
I answer his questions
as honestly as I need to,
but I'm hardly telling the town cop
what I do away from school.
That's my secret.

"I caught the evening train,
same as always,
to stay with my mother.
She's getting on in years, you know.
No, I didn't see anyone else on the platform.
Yes, I know Taylors Bend.
Doesn't everyone?
It's a lovers' lane, or so they say.
Yes, I've been there.
Alone.
I take a book and read,
enjoying the outdoors.

It's good for the health,

even in this gritty town.

No, I haven't been there this week.

I had dinner on Friday at the Sunset Café

and I caught the train to be with ...

"What!

You want her phone number?

What is going on, sir?

I don't want you disturbing her.

Look, I'm not answering another question.

What happens in the city is private.

Between my mother and myself.

It's not for anyone in this town to know about.

That is the end of the matter."

Sergeant Grainger

Butcher is a snob.
You don't need police training to see that.
He almost had a fit
when I suggested phoning his mother.
The old dear is probably as pompous
and insufferable as her son.
No doubt I'll get a lecture in manners
from the old woman as well.
Bugger it.
I'll look up Mrs. Butcher
in the phone book.
A cold call should put the wind up her son,
the stupid wowser.
Butcher's respected in town.
Not liked, but respected.
That won't stop Frank though.
If he hears I'm suspicious of anyone,
he'll beat the daylights out of them.
I've got a few days
before Frank and his mates
start getting pushy.
I don't want them deciding who's guilty.
A vein throbs in my temple
like a loud ticking clock.

Albert Holding

I came out here for a smoke
and to get away from the wife.
She's been on and on about the pub,
the beer,
my mates and me getting drunk
ever since the war.
War!
What does she know about it?
To blokes like Frank it meant starvation
and brutality beyond imagining.
He once told us, over a few beers too many,
that the lucky ones were those who died early.
The others came home to a life in the mines,
with nothing to look forward to but Friday afternoon
and a mate at the bar who understands.
He'd wake up at night to thunder,
thinking he's under attack
when it's only rain on the roof.
I spent too long in the desert driving trucks
when I could have been beside Frank
and had the honor of getting beaten to a pulp
by some slit-eyed bastard with a skeleton grin.

Some blokes reckon I was one step away
from a white feather in the mail.
Cheetham had his excuse,
being deaf in one ear.

But all I got was some pea-brain army doctor
scrawling "not for the frontline" on my report.
When I pushed the white ant for an answer
and stood close enough
for him to count my nose hairs,
he had the hide to say,
"It's not only the body that has to be fit, Holding."
I almost slugged him, then and there,
but they had military police
stationed outside his door.
He'd been punched a few times before
by the look of him.
Cheetham and me wandered around in a daze
for a week
until they stationed us in the Alice,
a million bloody miles from Frank and our mates.

When I got home
I thought the wife would understand
and wouldn't nag me
about going back down the mine,
where the enemy is a thousand tons of dirt
held up by timber studs and a few nails and bolts.
After the war I was going to make up for lost time.
But the time I spent away,
it's still lost.
No matter what I do,
it stays lost.
I pull hard on my durry

and watch the heavy clouds roll in.
It's going to rain for Colleen's funeral.
As it should.
At least that'll keep my wife quiet,
for an hour or two.

After the funeral.
That's when I'll make my move.
If Grainger can't put two and two together,
then I'll do it for him.
No one in this town will think of me as gutless.
Not this time.

FIVE | Burning Candles

Eddie

The Catholic church is full to bursting
with every pew taken
and people crowded along the walls
and at the back.
They shut the mine for a shift,
and the shops are all closed.
The school has a day off,
and we're spending it here with Colleen,
her coffin near the altar,
with a photo on top.
Her long blonde hair
shines from behind the glass,
and I can hear Mrs. O'Connor
crying in the front pew.
I'm wearing Dad's army boots,
polished with spit and rags,
because my feet are too big for my good shoes
and Dad said we weren't buying new ones,
not for a funeral.

Sally and me are sitting close,
listening to the priest
talk about God calling his children home,
welcoming them to his side,
asking us to pray for those lost
and those reunited.
I close my eyes

and imagine the river at Taylors Bend.
A bunch of us from school
went there one afternoon to swim.
Colleen sat on the wild grass beside the bank
and laughed as I dive-bombed from the tree
and nearly flooded the beach.

The priest asks us to stand
and hold hands to give us strength.
He prays that peace be with us,
and I'm pleased to feel Sally's warmth
and look into her sad eyes.
We sit down again and I glance around.
My family is in the pew opposite.
Larry is looking at the altar.
Mum is clenching her hands tight in her lap,
and Dad stares straight ahead,
not a muscle moving.
Mr. Carter is sitting near the front.
His paper said Colleen was a ray of sunshine
that bathed our town in a glow,
bright enough to stay with us forever.
When this is all over,
I'll thank him for honoring Colleen.
The priest calls us to sing,
but all I hear is the sound of hard rain
falling on my empty town.

Albert Holding

Christ Almighty!
I can't put up with this much longer.
The organ's grinding on,
putting my teeth on edge,
and the wife is crying by the bucketful.
If the rain crashes harder,
I won't have to hear this singing.
Paley's weaseled his way into the front pew,
wiping his pudgy face with a white handkerchief.
I remember him on Friday,
drunk and backslapping,
offering the shout.
I was outside under the sarsaparilla vine,
watching him buying friends at the bar,
until the girls came along,
and I turned my attention to them.
The town prays to a God
who takes young girls
and welcomes the killer into his church.
Believing,
it ain't worth a pinch of dust.

There's a trick I learned in the army,
on the parade ground
listening to the drill sergeant bellowing insults.
I stand straight and stare forward,
close my mind to everything,

feel my breathing steady,
and try to sleep, with my eyes open.
I spent long days at the base camp
working on doing nothing but this.
It's probably the only good thing I learned,
along with how to roll smokes with one hand
and how to hate someone
and never show it.

Mr. Butcher

Sergeant Grainger is up the back
looking for a sign, a weakness.
I dare not turn around to see him.
I stare straight ahead at the statue of Mary,
her immaculate heart,
and think of what to do.
But what I can't get out of my mind
is the sight of blonde hair
through my fingers.
I tighten with the memory.

Of course!
There's my answer.
I'll pay for a mother.
My blonde friend must have a mother,
or an aunt,
anyone who'll be Mrs. Butcher
if someone rings.
Simple.
A few pounds for answering a phone call.
I hope mother is like daughter,
willing to provide a service.
Anything to get rid of Grainger.
It's a waste of my wage though.
The money would be better spent
on soft warm silken pleasurable things.

Sally

As we follow the procession out of the church,
I want to hold Eddie's hand
but my dad is watching,
so I walk quietly beside him.
I hear his sharp intake of breath
as we see the rain falling on Colleen's coffin.
Mr. O'Connor and some miners
load the coffin into the wagon
for the short trip
around the corner to the cemetery.
We all follow in the rain.
Eddie opens an umbrella
and holds it over my head,
and instead of saying thanks,
I look at his downcast eyes
and say,
"I love you."

It just came out.
I looked into his eyes and saw love.
I thought I saw love,
so I mouthed the words.
The rain tumbles down
as we reach the old iron gates and file through.
Eddie's worth more than anything to me.
So I'm glad I said it.

Eddie

It's like the first time we kissed
beside the river
and I fled as fast as my feet could take me.
Only now,
I'm holding an umbrella
in a line of people.
There's no escape.
I focus on the hearse up ahead
and think of Colleen
being lowered into the ground.
I'm afraid of hearing
the thump of dirt on her coffin,
and her mother wailing
while Mr. O'Connor struggles
to hold himself steady.
Sally's words dance, uninvited,
inside my head.
I move the umbrella closer to Sally,
so I can feel the drops of rain
on my face,
cooling my skin
and rolling down my cheeks.
I feel too much.
Let the rain wash it away.

Mr. Carter

As the rain drenches us all,
I close my eyes for a minute
and pray for my Grace
to be with the young girl
and to tell her of our thoughts,
our sorrow,
and to forgive us.
The Lord sends these things
to test our spirit,
and while we can't make sense
or understand why,
we must believe and accept.

Mr. O'Brien leans heavily on his cane
beside the grave.
As we all start to leave,
I touch his arm and say,
"Can I walk with you, Bob?"
He was a watchmaker,
before the war, before his injury.
His workshop next to my office
rang with chimes and gongs,
and I marveled at his dexterity,
his long fingers tinkering
with the crowded workings
of all manner of clocks and watches.
We slowly file out of the cemetery,

his cane tapping a route home.

He says,

"Sometimes it's all right being the way I am.

Not having to see things."

When we reach his front gate,

he holds out his hand and asks,

"Are you still a Catholic, Mr. Carter?"

Before I answer,

he adds,

"If you are.

And I hope you are.

Burn a candle for Colleen

next time you're in church."

Eddie

Sally and me walk along the banks of the river
without saying a word.
Kingfishers and swallows,
creekdippers and acrobats,
swoop along the surface.
We duck under the branches of the willows
and cross the stream.
The water swirls around my knees
as I grip her hand.
We take nervous steps
through the cold rush,
our feet gripping the stones below.
When we reach the far bank,
I struggle out onto the high ground
and help her climb up the track.
On Jaspers Hill
we lie in the grass
under the cliffs,
away from town,
away from the memory of yesterday.
Sally kisses me
and I don't want to run this time.
I wrap my arms around her.
Then, in one quick movement,
Sally leans back and takes off her jumper,
tossing it behind her.
She's wearing a thin top

that clings to my fingers
as my hands drift over her body.
Sally grips my shoulders.
Her nails press into my skin
as she moves closer.
I smell her faint perfume,
feel her lips,
soft and welcoming.
My hands fumble under her blouse
exploring, awkward.
Her hand slips into my shirt
and I almost jump in fright.
I don't know what to do
with her fevered skin tingling
under my big clumsy hands.
She takes my hand,
placing it between her legs,
and the shock of her warmth
surges through me.
She pushes me back
and we are rubbing, touching, fondling,
doing things I've only dared think about.
Sally's breathing, my hands,
her lips, her face, her skin,
her smell, her touch,
fill my afternoon.

Albert Holding

The pub is quiet
with me and Johnno the bartender,
alone,
drinking the bitter brew of a desolate afternoon.
I told Laycock I was finishing early
and walked off before he could respond.
There's nothing at home for me.
I'm holding a glass of the only friend I've got.
Johnno sips his beer
and rabbits on about last Friday
and how everyone drank far too much,
and when Sergeant Grainger came in on Saturday
asking him to name the drunks,
Johnno scoffed and said,
"Every bloke in town, mate."
So we're all suspects, I guess.
I lean close to Johnno,
raise my glass,
swill it down,
and say, "Thanks.
One more for the guilty."
He looks at me in horror.
"Guilty of being drunk on Friday, you drongo."
He pours another as Fatty comes through the door,
looking pale and bloated,
like a fish tossed up on the bank.
He puffs,

"Just a shandy for me, thank you."
He sits beside me at the bar
and starts on.
"I'm so sorry for the parents.
It's a bad business for Burruga.
A blight on our future, you could say."

I down my beer in one gulp,
and say,
"There's only one bloke who can make it right,
Fatty."
I leave my money on the counter
and walk out.

Sergeant Grainger

The clock ticks past two in the morning
and the kettle boils on the stove.
Another cup of tea is better than sleep.
I've had a week of stories:
beer on Friday till closing,
rude singing, bad jokes,
and staggering home to a cold dinner
and an angry missus.
Some blokes want to take up a collection
for the O'Connors,
to help with the expenses,
and they asked me to look into it.
Everyone mentions how pretty Colleen was.
They didn't see her like me,
at the end,
on the sand.
That's what I can't shake.
It keeps me awake,
going over every detail.
Particularly the Holding family.
No one saw Eddie on Friday night,
and all he told me
is he sat up a tree beside the railway station
watching Butcher run late for the train.
So if I believe Eddie,
I should talk to Butcher again
and make more calls to the city.

Still no mother.

Albert Holding was as hostile as always.

He scowled at each question,

answered with a grunt whenever possible,

and looked off into the distance.

But when I mentioned Larry

he spat on the footpath, growling,

"No son of mine would do that.

The bloke who did it was gutless.

A coward.

That's who you should be looking for, Grainger. A coward."

Eddie

When Butcher calls her name I stand quickly,
my arm blocking the aisle.
Everyone looks at me.
Mr. Butcher sees his chance.
"I said 'Sally,' Eddie,
You don't look like Sally.
She's much prettier."
He's so proud of himself
when he hears the sly giggles.
It's all I can do to stop myself
from storming to his desk.
"Do you like pretty girls, sir?"
The laughter stops
and I hear my brother curse under his breath.
Butcher grabs his cane,
pointing to the door.
"Outside, Holding.
Not another word!"
I walk out slowly,
taking each deliberate step
with my eyes never leaving Butcher.
His hand is shaking and he shouts at the class.
"Chapter 4.
There'll be questions when I return."
Butcher leads me to the staff room.
"In here, boy."
He adjusts his glasses

and motions for me to hold out my hand.

"No, Mr. Butcher."

"What do you mean, Holding?

Don't disobey me."

I take a step toward him

and he starts to raise the cane.

"I know what happens in the city."

He steps back.

"What? What do you mean?"

I've been thinking of what to say,

careful not to accuse him of what I suspect.

"You won't choose Sally,

or any of the other girls to run errands for you.

From now on, choose a boy.

My brother, Larry, he'll do."

Butcher's face goes red with rage.

He taps the cane hard against his leg.

"Sergeant Grainger knows you almost missed the

train.

You can tell him what else happened."

Butcher says,

"There's nothing wrong in what I did.

Nothing whatsoever.

She's a fine young lady.

In fact, I'd call her my friend."

I open the door and walk back to class.

Butcher won't ridicule me again.

Mr. Carter

The week stumbles along
with everyone in town quiet, subdued.
The men walk home from the mine in groups.
No one stops at the pub.
They carry their lunchboxes
swinging by their sides,
and their heavy boots tramp down Main Street.
Everyone keeps their head bowed
as if they're scared they'll see the killer
in the eyes of a neighbor.
The O'Connor house has a For Sale sign out front,
and we're all doing our best not to notice it.
I've taken to sitting in the Sunset Café,
stirring my tea slowly,
looking for solace
somewhere between the Bible
and Banjo Paterson.
Unless Pete Grainger finds the guilty soon,
I fear the angry silence will snap,
with a horde of miners looking for retribution.
Mrs. Kain is quiet as she stands behind the counter
wiping the perfectly clean bench top.
Her eyes drift to the door,
and it hurts me to realize
she waits to see Colleen walk through the entrance,
smiling and ordering a milkshake.

Mr. Carter

Eddie Holding buys a bottle of milk
and walks across to my corner booth,
looking at my books on the table.
"Sit down, young fellow.
You're making me nervous."
He shakes his head
and glances to see if Mrs. Kain is listening.
"Thanks for what you wrote, Mr. Carter.
About Colleen.
It needed to be said."
He shuffles from foot to foot,
eager to leave.
"Why, thank you, Eddie.
Can I buy you a milkshake?
Please, take the weight off."
I gesture to the booth
and I'm about to call to Mrs. Kain
when Eddie interrupts.
"No, sir."
He holds up the bottle.
"Dad will need this when he gets home."
He walks to the door, stops and comes back,
"I wasn't saying it for a reason, Mr. Carter.
So you'd think better of me.
It was good someone wrote those things
about Colleen.
All everyone says is how pretty she was.
Not everything else."

Eddie walks down Main Street,
and I can't help but smile.
Praise be!
A Holding, of all people,
makes me proud to live in this town.
I open the notebook
with my list that fills two pages
and draw a line through Eddie's name.

Sally

Eddie and I share our sandwiches
and ignore everyone sniggering
and talking about us.

After what we did on Jaspers Hill
I've decided—no more hiding,
no more worrying what this town thinks.
We might die tomorrow.
I want to be with Eddie,
our legs touching on the seat.
God can't condemn something that feels so right.

I've watched my school friends
arguing over who was Colleen's best friend,
each trying to claim some memory.
And I've heard the rumors about Colleen
and a secret boyfriend,
meetings at the river.
It made my head swirl
because it's not true.
It's just inventions by people
scared to admit there's a killer in town.
Colleen didn't have a boyfriend.
She had a stalker.

Eddie

I've started going out after sunset,
wandering the town
between Main Street,
where Mr. Butcher lives,
and Sally's place.
I keep my eyes and ears open,
staying away from the light,
making sure I'll see him first.
Sometimes I hide in the bushes near the park
and sit for ages,
waiting,
expecting he'll walk by,
so I can follow him
and expose him.
If Sergeant Grainger doesn't find the killer,
we'll all go on living with this
and I'll spend my whole life
watching Mr. Butcher,
suspecting,
but never knowing.

Sergeant Grainger

My phone calls found only two families
related to Butcher.
One of them was a cousin
who told me that Butcher's mum died years ago
and they never see him anymore.
To quote,
"He lives in some God-forsaken dump
and doesn't come into the city."
I told the plonker he was wrong on both counts
and hung up.

There's a chap who stares at me
in my bathroom mirror
with bags under his eyes,
lines across his forehead,
hair getting thin on top.
He looks a hell of a lot like me,
only a fair bit older.

Mr. Butcher leaves for school at eight.
Today, he'll be late.

Sergeant Grainger

Butcher keeps looking downstairs
as we stand in his flat.
He doesn't offer me a seat.
"I was sorry to hear about your mother."
He almost drops his hat,
nervously fiddling with the brim.
A group of schoolchildren
call to each other on the footpath below.
"What did that Holding boy tell you?
I will not be intimidated.
That boy should be charged for threatening me."
He steps forward, raising his voice.
"So what if I have someone in the city?
If a man has to pay for a touch of female company,
it's no one's business."
I had a shower this morning,
but may need another
after I've finished with this grubby man.
"You were rushing for the train on Friday."
His eyes dart to the street below
as if the town can hear what I've said.
"Not especially."
The longer I keep silent,
the more he'll talk.
"Ernie Kain burned my grill.
You know how Mrs. Kain never shuts up,
well, they both forgot the food.

Kain insisted on cooking me a new dinner.

By the time I finished,

I had to run for the train."

He puts his hat on

and picks up his bag.

"That Holding boy had no right, no right whatsoever

to follow me."

Stepping in front of him, I say,

"When this is over,

I expect you'll leave town.

One way or the other."

I don't want him teaching our children.

"How dare you ..."

I move aside.

"Eddie isn't the only one watching you.

Understand?"

He looks like he does.

Larry

Sergeant Grainger waits in the park
near the school, watching.
He calls me over
before I jump the fence.
He nods for me to sit beside him.
"I'll be late for school, Sarge."
He scoffs and says,
"I'll give you a note for Butcher, if you like."
We both listen to the kids playing red rover.
"You got drunk on Friday, Larry."
He's not telling me anything.
"So did half the town, Sarge."
He flicks at a speck of dust on his trousers,
fingering the stiff crease.
"You and Eddie have been hunting before.
Right?"
What's he getting at?
"Sure. Rabbits for food.
No law against that, is there?"
He turns to face me
and stares until I can't look him in the eye.
"So you've seen a dead animal, Larry?"
"Who hasn't?" I shrug.
He waits a long time before speaking.
"Let me tell you this.
It's not the same as a human.
A young girl.

Someone who laughed
and maybe sang when they were alone,
sure no one could hear.
Or walked down Main Street
thinking of what she might do
when she got home.
You know, listen to the radio
or read a book.
Maybe sit in the sun
and feel its warmth."
My hands are shaking
as I remember Colleen in the library
and what I used to imagine.
Sergeant Grainger stands
and looks across at the school.
"When you've seen that, Larry.
It stays with you for ever."

SIX

Cowards

Sergeant Grainger

I drop by the *Guardian* office
on my way home.
Mr. Carter offers me tea
and ginger nut biscuits.
We sit in the old lounge chairs
at the front of the shop,
watching the miners walk past.
"Those men won't wait much longer," I say.
He closes the door,
shutting out the noise of the printing press
in the back room.
"I've made a list, Mr. Carter.
In five days, I haven't got very far."
I place my notebook on the coffee table,
open at the names.

Mr. Butcher.
Albert Holding.
The Johnston brothers.
Larry Holding.
Other teenage boys?

He reads the names and smiles.
"I've made my own list, Pete."
He taps the notebook in his shirt pocket.
"You know,
Eddie Holding came up to me

at the Sunset Café yesterday

and thanked me

for writing Colleen's obituary.

As he walked out,

I had a hunch

that it's not a young bloke.

It's a man.

You're looking for a man, Pete.

Not much of one, I admit.

But it's not a boy."

I sip my tea,

wishing for something stronger.

"Albert Holding says I'm looking for a coward."

Mr. Carter heaps a spoon with sugar

and watches it slide into his tea.

He takes a long time to answer.

"Albert's no fool.

He could be right."

We sit in silence,

watching the sun set

and the streetlights flicker on.

"How many cowards do we have in town, Pete?"

That's easy to answer.

"One.

One too many."

Sergeant Grainger

An icy breeze blows down from the hills.
The pub is deserted,
like it's been all week.
Albert Holding sits alone.
I step inside and feel the warmth of the fire.
When I was a young lair
the front bar and me were best mates.
Albert's eating hot chips,
adding extra salt from the shaker.
He sees me enter and nods.
I order a beer and offer Albert a refill.
"Sure. A copper buying beers.
I wouldn't knock that back."
There's no reason to tiptoe around him.
"I reckon you're right, Albert.
A coward.
That's who I'm looking for."
He takes another chip
and swallows it in one bite.
"Look, Sarge.
It ain't Larry.
If a son of mine did that,
well …
you wouldn't need to lock him away.
He'd be dead."
It's obvious he doesn't know about Eddie
following Butcher into the city.

If I told him that,
he'd flatten Butcher with one punch
and then do the same to his son
for nicking off.
I'll keep my silence, for now.
"You don't need to go picking on my boy.
Open your eyes."
He wipes the salt from his mouth
with the back of his sleeve.
"Cowards don't always hide.
Sometimes, they're so gutless
they need to stand out.
You know what I mean?"
Holding looks at me,
to make sure I understand.
I scull my beer,
say good-bye,
and step into the cutting wind
that almost blows my hat down lonely Main Street.
The cryptic bastard is playing me for a fool.

Larry

Mates at school called my dad a chicken
for refusing to go down the mine
and earn a real wage.
All he did in the war was drive trucks.
While they talked about their dads
lost in the jungle somewhere
or captured by the Japs,
me and Eddie kept quiet
about Dad on some highway up north.
Since the funeral,
Dad's the only one who stops at the bar.
The other men buy a bottle or two
and take them home in a brown paper bag,
to be with their family.
Not Dad.
He sits at the bar,
like nothing's happened,
like nothing's changed.
Everyone's saying what a cold bastard he is.
I'm sitting opposite the pub,
smoking a fag,
waiting to walk home with him.
When he comes out he sees the durry.
"Beer and smokes.
They'll both kill ya, son."
He's not the cheeriest bloke in town.
"Better than dying of boredom, Dad."
Geez, I almost got a laugh out of him then.

"No one at the pub again tonight?"

He takes his hat off

and bends the brim back into shape,

pulling it low over his eyes.

He says,

"All that beer going to waste.

Someone's gotta keep Johnno company."

I say,

"I reckon it takes a lot of guts

to do something no one else will do."

Dad stops and tries to get my meaning.

"You saying your dad's got guts, son?"

"Sure. Why not."

He stops and shakes his head.

"Do me a favor, Larry.

Head on home and tell your mum

I'll be a little late, okay?"

He starts walking back to the pub

even though it's closing time.

Mum will be as mad as hell.

And me?

I'll be an old man myself

before I understand one thing about my father.

Eddie

I know their names off by heart,
from the First World War.
Sixteen blokes from the area died
and the town lays wreaths once a year
for their supreme sacrifice.
I'm sitting beside the white stone memorial
at the top of Main Street.
It's cloudy tonight,
and I can smell the rain blowing in.
Footsteps echo down the street.
A man in an old jacket and khaki trousers
walks through the alley,
a hat shielding his face.
He lights a cigarette
and flicks the match into the gutter
as he walks toward Valley Road,
where Sally lives.
I wait until he turns the corner,
then I sneak from the memorial and follow.
My head is spinning.
It can't be *him*.

He's out for a walk,
nothing more.
Innocent.
Totally innocent.
He moves ahead of me,
like he knows where he's going.

I close my eyes and hope
he'll go into another street
before he reaches Sally's place.
He passes Wheelers Lane,
Brunton Street,
and stops opposite Valley Road.
He stubs the cigarette out with his boot,
walks across the bitumen,
and disappears out of sight.
I run as fast as I can,
afraid I'll lose him,
and equally afraid
I won't.

There he is.
Standing under the streetlamp, looking at each of the houses
on the high side of Valley Road,
right near Sally's.
He stays there for a long time,
his hands in his pockets,
not moving or calling out.
Just standing.
Then he walks down the road
before entering the bush
and heading home.
I kick the hard ground
and the dirt flies from my boots.
Why didn't I have the guts
to move out from the shadows
and let him see me?

Albert Holding

The frost in the air
settles in my bones.
I don't know what I'm doing here,
what I'm expecting to happen.
I look at all the houses
on the poshest street in town.
Their gardens are neat,
the trees pruned,
the driveways swept of leaves.
I can smell the woodsmoke from the chimneys.
Each house has a painted timber fence
with a shiny silver gate, shut.
The lawns are like carpet,
and a concrete path leads to the steps
and the brightly painted doors.
I live in a crumbling shack
me and the boys built,
with three rooms for four people.
I light another cigarette
and stand outside his house.
In the army,
fights were as common as parade drills,
only much more satisfying.
My fists haven't had a good workout in years.

Mr. Butcher

I board the train
in the early evening
and it's empty, as usual.
We slowly pass farms with run-down fences
and wind-beaten houses.
There's nothing worth staying for in this town.
They can all go to hell.
I'll get another job
in a place far away,
where I'm appreciated for my teaching.
I'll forget what happened here.
Tonight, alone on the platform
as the train pulled in,
I heard a voice shouting at me.
Angry, strangled,
threatening across the fields.
My legs almost buckled as I opened the door
and stepped into this lonely carriage.
Burruga is cursed, haunted.

I take out pencil and paper
and start drafting a letter of resignation.
It's brief and to the point.
First thing Monday morning.
I don't care if it looks suspicious.
No one can stop me leaving.
I pat the wallet in my breast pocket

and hope I have enough money
for tonight and tomorrow.
I need comfort, release,
a distraction,
to help me forget.

Mr. Carter

It was late at night
when I heard the footsteps
outside my bedroom window.
Albert Holding stood
looking up at the houses.
He was there for a long time
staring at the Holmes house,
or the Paley place.
I couldn't tell which.
He wasn't trying to hide.
He was very still, watching,
almost wanting to be seen.

This morning
I think of telling Mr. Holmes,
or Mayor Paley,
about their visitor,
until I realize that Eddie and Sally
are friends, good friends.
Perhaps that's it?
But why would Albert
not want Eddie and Sally …
it doesn't make sense.

I walk slowly into town
going over it in my mind.
Albert's not the type

to worry about his boys with a girl.
They can look after themselves.

And then it hits me.
Good Lord.

Mayor Paley

That bloody Holding has a nerve,
hanging about my house last night.
I have a right to call Grainger
when I get into the office this morning,
have him warn Holding about loitering
like a common thief.

Wilma hands me my lunch
and kisses me on the cheek.
Well, let Holding come back tonight,
and every night,
for all I care.
He doesn't worry me.
I'll do what I did last night:
close the curtain,
pour myself a strong scotch
with no ice,
and drink it in one gulp.
It calms me down.

Eddie

Sally and I start the long climb
up to Jaspers Hill.
I lead her along the narrow track,
overgrown with the banksia and honeysuckle.
We step over rabbit holes
and wallaby droppings.
A chicken hawk fluttering like a kite
casts a perfect shadow across the path.
All our effort is on reaching the top
where the sun heats the granite rocks.
When we finally make it,
we're both sweating.
I lean back against the smooth boulders,
and Sally looks over the town.
"It seems so small from up here."
She sits beside me
and her hair falls in front of her face.
She leans forward
and wraps the thick locks in her hands,
folding them into a shiny knot.
A long vein throbs in the milk skin of her neck.
She says,
"It's good to be away from everyone.
I can't believe some of the rumors."
Then she looks embarrassed.
"About Colleen. Not us."
Sally asks,

"Do you think they'll find who did it?"
I reach for her hand
and pull her gently toward me.
The only answer I can find is to kiss her
and try to forget what I saw last night.
She leans across me and smiles.
"We're all alone …"

Mr. Carter

Mrs. Kain comes in early

with a classified she wants me to run.

For a while

I'm distracted from my suspicions.

Who do I tell?

Pete Grainger?

Or should I talk to Albert first?

Get some idea why he was standing there.

Or Paley?

Could it be?

The sleep of an honest man is sweet,

the torture of the guilty, endless.

I raise the blinds in the office

and watch the ladies going into the emporium.

Our mayor.

When I was young

my mother always said,

"The more money, the more lies."

It's why I became a newspaperman.

The truth.

And now, do I know the truth?

I place my cup in the sink,

reach for my jacket and my hat.

When I close the door behind me,

I turn to lock it, then decide not to.

It's time to start trusting my town again.

I walk down the street to the police station.

Eddie

After I take Sally home,
I wander to Taylors Bend,
where Colleen died.
No one comes here anymore.
But I have to.
It's just a river
where we dived and swam.
The evil is not here.
I hear a shuffling of feet
on the track behind me.
It's Barney Haggerty.
He stops and looks at me,
trying to remember my name.
"I'm Eddie, Mr. Haggerty."
He takes a swig of metho
and sways slightly.
He says,
"I just saw your dad,
walking by the train tracks."
My dad should be at work.
Maybe Mr. Haggerty's had a few too many.
"Carrying a bloody big rope, he was."
He shakes the bottle,
checking there's some left
before taking another mouthful.
"I asked for a few bob.
You know, to tide me over."

He grins at me and winks.

"He's a good bloke."

Mr. Haggerty turns around

like an unsteady sailor,

arms reaching to grab some imaginary rail,

and walks up the track back into the hills.

Eddie

For a few minutes I can't move,
going over in my brain,
trying to imagine what Mr. Haggerty saw.
I head for home, slowly,
wondering why Dad would need a thick rope.
Maybe Laycock has a cow caught in a bog
and Dad's got a rope from the mine to help?
I follow the river for a while.
In the shallows,
a trout twists against the flow,
waiting for an insect to break the surface.
Maybe Dad could use some help?
If it's one of Laycock's bulls,
they'll need as many hands as possible.
I spin and run back down the track,
even though I'm probably on a wild-goose chase
looking for Haggerty's ghost.

Round the bend I see Dad,
in the distance,
with his hands on his hips,
looking across the river
to the railway bridge.
I can see the shape
of a man on the bridge.
A big man.

Albert Holding

I couldn't wait any longer.
George Weaver told me yesterday
he'd visited Frank and Betty.
He said Betty refuses to leave the house
and wastes all day sitting in the kitchen
shelling peas, peeling spuds,
and cooking meals neither of them want to eat.
Frank spends most of the daylight in the shed,
standing at the bench,
rearranging his tool shelves
and trying to keep himself busy.
George shook his head and said,
"All those years the Japs couldn't kill him.
And now this."

Bugger the consequences!
This morning I marched into Fatty's shop,
along the rows of brand-new overalls
and kettles and boilers and saucepans
and more boots and shoes
than I'll ever be able to afford.
One of the workers
tried to stop me going up the stairs to his office,
but I pushed him aside.
"I have an appointment," I said.
Yeah, one that Fatty doesn't know about yet.
He jumped to his feet when I came in.

"What is this, Holding?"

His turkey chin kept shaking after he spoke.

"You did it, Fatty."

He tried to bluff his way through the moment,

accusing me of being rude,

looking nervously around for someone to help.

"What are they going to do, Fatty?

Make me leave?

You've had long enough.

Now I'll go straight to Grainger

and he can sort it."

His eyes clouded over

and his fat, wobbly legs started shaking.

He could see I meant what I said.

"You've got until one o'clock.

That's longer than you deserve."

Looking at him made me sick.

I spat on his desk,

on the papers and the folders

he's spent his life hiding behind.

"This afternoon.

At the bridge over the river, Fatty.

You know where that is, don't you?

Meet me there, or go to Grainger

and see if you can bullshit your way past him.

It's your choice.

You'd be smarter choosing the copper, Fatty."

Then I walked out of his neat little office

straight to the hardware counter

and bought some rope.
For once I didn't mind spending money
in Fatty's shop.
I kept moving all morning,
trying to decide what I'd do if he showed.
Would I have enough guts to end it?

Mayor Paley

The temerity of the man.
Accusing me!
I … I … I shouldn't have to face
such vile slandering.
The insolent way he called me
Fatty was beyond the pale.
I told him,
"My name's Kenneth.
Or Mr. Paley to you."
I tried to explain …
He was wrong.
Why would I …
My hands were shaking,
and I could barely control my legs.
He threatened me.
I'm … I'm … I'm … the mayor.
No one gives me orders.

When he left my office,
I slumped back in my chair,
gripping the desk.
What can I do?
What can I do?

Eddie

Mr. Paley is on the bridge,
pleading.
The thick rope is around his neck,
circles his hands,
goes down to the tracks
and under the wooden sleeper.
My dad stares across at the bridge
and reaches into his pocket,
taking out his smokes.
He casually begins rolling a fag
as if he's got all day.
Mr. Paley shouts something
I can't hear over the swirling water.
Then he drops to his knees.
Is he crying?
Or praying?
Why isn't Dad going to help?
He's just cupping his hands
as he lights his smoke
in the shade of a tree
beside the river.

Albert Holding

He's not going to jump until he has to.
I know Fatty.
There were blokes like him in the army,
working in stores,
loading ships,
doing anything to avoid fighting.
All of us cowards
got the cushy home jobs
while men like Frank went off
and faced their own tortures,
for mongrels like Fatty and me.
You could pick us out
when we returned home.
We talked louder
and exaggerated our piddling little army jobs
or trotted out excuses about physical defects
and doctor's orders stopping us from fighting.
All bullshit.
Cowards and bullshit.
They're best mates.

I know Fatty
because
I know myself.

There he is,
whimpering,

blubbering.

I think of that poor girl

and what he must have done.

My hands are steady,

solid as a rock

when I light the cigarette.

The rope flexes.

Cheetham's knot works.

Fatty can't escape.

The more he struggles,

the tighter it gets.

"It's your choice, Fatty."

I hope for his sake he jumps

and tests the strength of the rope.

Maybe it won't hold

and he'll fall into the river below.

Then we'll let Frank take care of him.

But for Colleen's sake,

I hope he stands there and faces the train

and gets wiped out.

Disappears.

I flick the cigarette

and watch it get sucked under the whirlpool.

Not long now.

Mayor Paley

I tried to tell him it was a misunderstanding.
The young girl was laughing.
I thought she was interested.
I was drunk!
For God's sake!
When I tried to kiss her
she backed away into the bushes.
I followed.
Maybe I grabbed at her skirt and pulled.

Holding punched me!
While I was dazed he tied my hands
and shackled me to this.

"Let me go!
I'm the mayor, you know.
What if a train comes?"

What happened with the girl was an accident!
She tried to run past me
and I grabbed her again.
I didn't know what I was doing.
She screamed.
I thought she'd wake the neighborhood.
The look of disgust on her face!
Didn't she know who I was?
Once!

Only once I slapped her.
She stumbled and fell.
Her head hit a rock.
A horrid sound.
If only she hadn't struggled.
I wasn't going to hurt her.

When I saw the blood …
There was nothing more I could do.
An accident.

"This is an outrage.
Untie these ropes!
Now!"

Eddie

Suddenly, I hear the train whistle
in the distance.
Mr. Paley screams.
He's shaking the rope
side to side.
Frantic.
He's running on the spot,
trying to free himself from the noose.
Dad points up the tracks
and shouts across to Mr. Paley,
"It's your choice, Fatty."
The whistle answers
and I know the coal train
will soon be bearing down on Mr. Paley.

I plunge into the water.
It's so cold,
my breath catches in my throat.
Maybe I can get there
and loosen the rope
before the train.
Dad shouts something
as I struggle to the bank
and start climbing.
"I'm coming, Mr. Paley."
I grab tufts of weeds to pull myself up,
my feet digging into the soft soil,

scrambling with every ounce of effort.

Mr. Paley is shouting,

"Hurry up, boy. Help!

For heaven's sake!"

I reach the track

and see the coal train rounding the bend.

Dad screams from the bank,

"Jump, you coward.

Jump!"

Eddie

Jump?

Is Dad yelling at me?

The water surges below.

My legs balance, wobble, step.

If my feet miss the sleepers

I'll be trapped with Mr. Paley.

The train is thundering toward the bridge.

I can see the driver

blowing his whistle,

pulling the emergency brake.

He's shouting,

but all I can hear is the furious screeching

of wheels on the track.

I leap over three sleepers at a time,

reaching out to Mr. Paley

even though I'm still too far away.

"STOP!"

Mr. Paley twists to face the train.

He flings his hands up

as if he can stop it.

"NO!"

He jumps

and I throw myself after him.

I grab nothing but air,

falling,

my arms flailing.

The river rushes to meet me.

Eddie

In my dream
I'm fourteen years old
and Dad is wearing his army uniform,
with boots and buttons polished.
Mum, Larry, and me are waiting at the platform.
Dad jumps from the train
before it stops
and wraps his big arms around me.
I can smell his tobacco breath
and feel the tingling prickle of his stubble.
Although he still has his duffle bag
slung over one shoulder,
he's so strong he lifts me in a bear hug,
grinning and saying,
"It's good to be home."
We walk across town.
I'm carrying his bag
and he's holding Mum's hand.
Our shack by the river
is covered in streamers to welcome him.
People from town visit all afternoon
to say hello and thank him for what he did.
Everyone points to the sign I painted
over the front door.
For my dad.
Who fought in the war,
side by side with Frank O'Connor.

Deep in the jungle,
with the enemy all around.
In my dream.

Eddie

I wake in bed
and my head is throbbing so much
it hurts to open my eyes.
Mum's voice comes from under the door.
"You had no right!
To put your son in danger like that …"
I try to get up,
but dizziness overwhelms me.
I lie back
and wait for a few minutes
until I can open my eyes again.
All I remember is jumping
and the train driver's face twisted in agony
as I fell,
and he reached out the window,
a despairing arm,
trying to catch me,
but I kept falling.

Then I remember.
I fell past Mr. Paley.

The rope held.
The mayor is dead.
For all I know he's still there
swinging below the bridge.
I couldn't save him.

I squeeze my eyes tight
to stop myself seeing his face.
Roaring in my head
is the certainty that I failed.
I stuff the sheet into my mouth
and bite down hard
to stop myself from screaming.

Albert Holding

Eddie rushed across the river,
and my guts tightened
like I'd been punched.
I knew what he was going to do.
Even if he could make it to Paley
he'd never free the rope in time.
Not before the train.
I shouted with all the venom I felt
for Fatty to jump
and spare my son.
My son's life
in the hands of a coward.

Fatty waited until it was too late.
I closed my eyes,
unable to watch
as the train stormed past.
I was on my knees
beating my fists on the ground,
sure that Fatty had not only killed Colleen
but now he'd taken my son.
Then I saw him.
Eddie had jumped.
He was facedown in the water
near the bank.
I dragged him out,
crying,

calling his name over and over,
afraid he couldn't hear me,
would never hear me again.
He whispered something.
Someone's name.
I carried him up the track to our house.
My son in my arms.
As I reached the bend,
I looked back.
Paley was hanging from the bridge,
the rope swinging tight,
his eyes lifeless,
staring straight across the water
at me.

SEVEN

The Bridge

Sergeant Grainger

Albert is in the yard
swinging his ax,
splitting firewood.
He sits on the chopping block
and rolls a smoke,
offering me the packet
as he shields his eyes
from the setting sun.
"Do you know Mr. Paley is dead?"
He shrugs and drags deeply on the cigarette,
letting the smoke drift away.
I say,
"It must have taken a lot of guts
to do what Mr. Paley did.
To jump with a rope around his neck."
Albert looks up fiercely,
as though he wants to shout,
but he stops himself.
I almost had him.

All I have to do is keep baiting him
and he'll crack.
He'll tell me what I want.
What I suspect.
Paley wasn't alone.
How could he tie his own hands?
I say,

"Mr. Paley did a lot for this town, Albert.

When all you men were away.

He worked tirelessly for the war effort.

Raising money. Organizing."

Albert stabs the cigarette into the block,

crushing it in his fingers.

A voice behind me says,

"Mr. Paley jumped, sir."

Eddie is near the clothesline,

hands in his pockets.

His hair is messy,

and he looks unsteady on his feet.

"I was there, sir.

I saw what happened."

He walks to the woodpile

and stands beside his father.

Eddie's eyes are bloodshot,

and his dad can't meet his gaze.

"I tried to stop him …"

Tears fill Eddie's eyes.

Should I ask him if anyone else was there?

He'll tell me the truth.

But I already have the answer.

I place my hand on Eddie's shoulder.

"Thanks, son.

You did your best."

I nod to Albert

and take my leave.

There's no point in pressing Eddie.

He did what he could,

and that was more than enough.

Mr. Carter

On my desktop calendar,
Galatians reads:
For every man shall bear his own burden.
And mine is to sit here
without typing a word.
I notice the spider web
hanging from the ceiling.
A huntsman scurries across the wall.
There's so much to write
and I can't print a word of it.
Headlines flash through my mind,
"Mayor Commits Suicide."
"Murder Solved." Simple.
To the point.
An end to all the rumors.
Except there's no proof.
I'm not printing gossip.
Or theories.
I'm not calling a dead man
a murderer.
Not on the front page of the *Guardian*.
Wilma Paley is beside herself with grief.
I type:
The mayor of Burruga, Mr. Kenneth Paley,
was found dead near Jamison River.
Sergeant Grainger has yet to make a statement
regarding the cause of death.
All of Burruga will mourn this tragic loss of life.

The rest of the article comes automatically.

Mr. Paley's past.

His achievements.

I finish with the line:

Mr. Paley is survived by his loving wife, Wilma.

I'm glad they didn't have children.

At the top of the page

I type the heading:

Tragic Death.

Enough said.

Eddie

Sergeant Grainger leaves,
and Dad goes back to chopping wood
as if nothing has happened.
I watch him split the ironbark
with clean, sharp blows.
He cuts much more than we need for tonight,
tomorrow,
the whole week.
He doesn't look at me.

"Dad."
He grips the ax and swings,
splitting the log in one clean blow.
"Take these logs in for your mother, Eddie."
I lean down,
then stop myself.
"No. Not yet."
He's going to have to tell me.
I stand in front of the chopping block
and reach for the ax in his hands.
"Look at me."
Dad's shoulders sag.
He glances back at the house
to see if Mum is watching.
My legs buckle and I feel dizzy
as I sit on the block.
Dad crouches beside me,

whispering urgently,

"Fatty killed Colleen.

The bastard murdered that girl,

and I wasn't going to let him get away with it."

I swallow hard to stop the bile rising.

"Why? How?

I mean, how do you know?"

Dad looks up sharply,

and he's about to snap at me.

Then he remembers what happened.

"I have a right to ask."

He covers his face.

I see the cuts and burns on his knuckles

from the heavy rope.

They must have fought on the bridge ...

"Grainger was asking questions, Eddie.

He suspected Larry.

People were talking about your brother

being drunk that night.

As if that made him guilty!

Larry can be a fool,

but he isn't a murderer.

I told Grainger the killer was a coward."

Dad looks blindly at the firewood

and the ax and says,

"The only cowards in town were Fatty and me."

My head is spinning.

Dad tied a rope around the mayor's neck

because he thought Mr. Paley was a coward?
"What about Butcher?"
Dad shrugs,
"He goes into the city on Friday nights."
I grab Dad's shirt and shake him
with all my strength, shouting,
"He was late for the train.
He was late for the train.
I saw him running!"

Dad shoves me back
and I tear his shirt.
The rip stops us both,
and we look at the cloth in my hands.
Dad says, "It was him, Eddie.
He admitted it.
As soon as the rope went around his wrists
he started gushing.
He was guilty as sin."

I don't want to hear any more.
I rush past Dad,
jump over the fence,
head into the bush.
I need to get as far away as I can.
Dad calls my name but I don't look back.

Eddie

By the time I reach the top of Jaspers Hill,
my breath is coming in short, sharp stabs.
I drop under the overhang of Coal Scar Man,
keeping my eyes closed,
trying to shut out what Dad has done.
Let me stay here forever.
I wrap my arms tight around my body
to ease the sobbing,
praying for rain to start
and never stop
until the valley is awash
and the river overflows
and covers our house,
the streets of my town,
and cleans away all that blood
from the sand where Colleen died
and floods the bridge where Mr. Paley …

I can see Mr. Paley
just before I got to him.
I remember now.
He said,
"Forgive me."
His eyes were calm.
He knew his fate.
He spun around to face the train.
We both jumped.

I reached out for him
and tried to take him with me,
but the rope held
and I kept falling
into the rushing water.

Maybe Dad was right,
but how could he be certain?
Unless he was there when Colleen …
"NO!
Please no."
My whole body starts shaking.
I'll have to face him.
My father.
Coward.

Sergeant Grainger

Mrs. Paley asked me to lock up when I leave.

The store will be closed for a few days,

in memory of Kenneth Paley.

Tonight I'm a cop in the mayor's office,

taking out one drawer at a time,

emptying the contents onto his desk,

making a right mess,

handling each object.

Staples, fountain pens,

notepads full of work orders,

pencils, sharpener,

paper and an invoice book.

As boring as bat shit.

But here, in the bottom drawer,

there's a green metal box,

locked.

Something moves inside when I shake it.

I could go downstairs to the shop,

grab a crowbar and snap the lock.

But cops aren't supposed to do that.

So I spend the next thirty minutes

searching for the bloody key,

going through each account book,

through each folder

in the whole bookcase.

I'm about to chuck the box against the wall

in the hope it might break open,

by accident, you understand,
when I remember the key chain on Paley's belt.
Mr. Smyth gave me all his possessions
to pass on to the widow.
I've been too busy chasing my tail to do it yet.
It's on my desk at home.

If there's anything to find,
it's in this box.

Sally

It's dark when I knock
at the Holding house,
quietly.
Quick footsteps,
Eddie's mum opens the door.
Her eyes search behind me.
"Have you seen him?"
She looks haunted.
"He's not here.
We don't know where he is."
She grabs my arm and pleads,
"You'll tell him to come home, won't you?
If you see him.
Please."
I nod quickly and leave.

Jaspers Hill?
There's just enough moonlight
to scramble up the track,
calling his name,
listening for an answer.
The rumors are sweeping town.
Eddie tried to save Mr. Paley
from jumping off the bridge.

Eddie is curled up on a rock,
head bowed,

hugging his knees, shivering.
I put my arms around him
and hold him until the lights of the mine
glow bright in the valley.
Two sharp siren calls
signal the end of dinner break.
There's nothing I can say.
I'm staying with Eddie
until he's ready to come down,
no matter how long it takes.

Sergeant Grainger

I have Mrs. Paley's permission to open the box.
"Do whatever you have to.
Find out what happened."
She meant something different
from what I was suspecting.

As kids, we used to search the river
for sunken treasure.
A bunch of us diving,
hands tracing the sandy bottom.
Once, we found the steering wheel
of a Bedford truck.
When I presented it to my father,
he grinned and tousled my hair.
"It'll come in handy, son.
If we find the rest of the truck."

I turn the key in the lock
and lift the lid.
A white cloth is wrapped around some items.
A broken wristwatch,
a school photo from this year,
a deck of smutty cards
with pictures of naked women,
and a bank book.
The last withdrawal was today.
Five hundred pounds.

Mr. Smyth gave me Paley's things in a satchel.

Keys, a wallet, cuff links,

and a sealed envelope.

It doesn't take a genius to work out what's inside.

I should pass this on to the widow.

But, for now, it's evidence.

Five hundred pounds worth of evidence.

Eddie

I tell Sally everything.
My dad, Mr. Paley, and Colleen.
She holds my hand and listens.
Sergeant Grainger will ask me
what went on at the bridge.
What can I say?
How can I face my dad again?
After what he did!
What will I tell Mum and Larry?
What if Mrs. Paley comes up to me in town
and thanks me for trying to save her husband?
That's when it hits me …

I wasn't just thinking of Mr. Paley.
When I came out of the bush,
I could see Dad
standing on the other side of the river,
smoking a fag
and watching.
I knew then
that if the train hit Mr. Paley
it would kill my dad,
sooner or later.
I was trying to save Dad,
but he didn't want to be saved.

Eddie

We make our way down from the hill,
across the paddocks to the bridge.
The river glides below.
"No matter how fast I ran,
it wouldn't have helped.
Mr. Paley knew there was no chance."
Sally reaches for my hand.
I kick a stone over the edge
and wait to hear it drop into the water.
A long way down.
"What Dad did was …"

A torchlight shines in my face,
and I step in front of Sally,
shielding my eyes.
Sergeant Grainger's voice calls,
"Sorry, Eddie. It's me and Mr. Carter.
Sally's parents were worried,
so I said we'd find her."
He switches off the light,
and I can make out two figures
standing on the riverbank.
"Don't worry, Sally.
I told them you were with Eddie.
You were safe."
Mr. Carter adds,
"Eddie. Why don't you come down and talk to us.

That bridge gives me the creeps."
There won't be a train until dawn,
so I motion for Sally to sit with me
on the railway track.

There are two men now as witness.
My words come slowly.
"Mr. Paley was roped to the bridge this afternoon
because of what he did to Colleen.
He came here because he was guilty."
Please, let that be the truth.
"He asked me to forgive him
and I wished I had time to,
before the train …
before it was too late."
Dark clouds press down on Jaspers Hill.
"So I want to say
that I forgive Mr. Paley
because there's nothing more
that can be done for him."
Both men are as silent as death.
My heart pounds wildly,
and I press my hand hard to my chest.
"Someone else was here.
Someone who knew about Colleen."

I hear footsteps
and see Dad walking along the bridge.
"I thought I'd find you here," he says.

My legs start to shake.
I don't know whether to run toward him
or away.

Albert Holding

On a railway bridge,
in the middle of the night.
It's as good a place as any
to tell them what I know.
"Fatty was drunk last Friday,
and he wandered out of the pub.
He bumped into me
and I wanted to deck him,
then and there.
But he was the mayor.
And me,
I'm just some bloke who went to war
and didn't see any fighting.
I wasted my time driving trucks
while Paley got fat and rich."
I look at Eddie,
hoping he'll understand.
"I was gonna knock Fatty down
and take his money,
the money he does nothing to earn,
sitting pretty up in his office
while the rest of us work.
Anyway, I followed him.
He stumbled along,
pissed as a parrot.
I'd had a few myself
and I needed to take a leak,

which made me lose sight of him.
So I sat down
and thought better of what I was doing.
Yeah, maybe I was spineless.
Afraid to take on Fatty Paley,
even when we're both stonkered.
Then I saw him stagger out of the bush.
He looked scared as hell,
cursing to himself.
So I went down the track.
That's when I saw the girl.
Colleen.
I knelt beside her.
It was too late.
Fatty was running home by now
as fast as his jelly legs could take him.
And I thought that if I told my story,
well, who would you believe?
Come on, Sergeant,
who would you believe?"

Only the river answers,
muttering darkly over the rocks.
"I thought I'd give it a week.
Fatty would break
and start blubbering to you, Sarge.
But he was a coward,
right to the end."

Eddie

Dad's shoulders drop,

and he rubs his hands roughly over his face,

shaking his head.

I move toward him,

my arms ready if he needs me.

"It's over, Dad."

He looks up

and says,

"No. Not yet."

He speaks to the men on the bank.

"I told Fatty he had a choice.

Either turn himself in,

or meet me here

and face the consequences.

That's what I said to him.

I gave him a few hours to think about it.

I didn't think he'd show.

And do you know what he did?"

Dad clenches his fists

and thumps his chest hard,

pushing the words out.

"He offered me money!

Five hundred pounds to forget about it.

Christ Almighty.

Five hundred pounds!

What man has that much money?

To buy the life of Frank's daughter!"

Dad takes a step forward,

looking down at the surging water.

He stiffens and shouts at Sergeant Grainger,

"I tied the rope around his neck

and through this sleeper here.

An army knot.

I knew Fatty wouldn't have the guts.

So I gave him no choice.

I helped him do what he couldn't do alone."

Mr. Carter

Pete touches my arm,

indicates we should leave,

without response.

We sleepwalk down the track toward town,

not using the torch.

Let the surrounding bush conceal us.

We stop at the sandy beach

where we found Colleen

and sit for a moment.

I say,

"He was telling the truth."

Pete reaches down to retie his shoelaces,

giving himself time to think.

"Thank Christ Albert didn't take the money."

I look at the scallop shapes

of too many footprints in the white sand.

It's a sin to lie,

but I pray He'll understand.

"On Monday, the front page will read,

'Mayor Commits Suicide.'"

It won't stop people from talking,

but at least,

on record,

we'll have a version we can all live with.

I'm going to print a falsehood.

"Tomorrow is Sunday, Pete.

Let Albert spend it with his family.

You can arrest him, Monday morning,

after the *Guardian* is out.

Paley jumped.

Albert just gave him the courage."

Eddie

Dad sags to his knees
and looks over the edge of the bridge
at the moon-slick water.
"Take Sally home, Eddie.
Don't let her parents worry any longer."

There's nothing more I can say,
it's all twisted and wrenched out of me.
Dad will always feel the rope in his hands,
cutting through the skin,
leaving a red welt.
No matter what he does from now on,
the blemish will be there.
A mark that no rain can wash off.
No soap,
no work on the farm,
no coal dust smeared across,
no cigarette stain will hide.

Mr. Paley jumped today
and so did Dad.

Eddie

Mr. Holmes is sitting on his front step
when we turn into his street.
He rushes to the gate.
Sally kisses me, quickly, on the cheek.
Mr. Holmes nods.
"Thanks for bringing her home, Eddie."
He puts his arm around Sally
as they walk up the stairs.
Next door the Paley house is dark,
windows and doors shut tight,
heavy curtains drawn.
No smoke rises from the chimney.

The man responsible waits at the bridge.
His blood is my blood.
He found Colleen,
touched her lifeless body.
Did he reach down and close her eyes?
He could have gone to Sergeant Grainger
and told him what he knew.
But he left her there,
for someone else to find.

My father walked around for days and did nothing.
He ate dinner with us.
Drank at the pub.
He slept beside Mum.

And told no one.
Did nothing until this.

I run to Sally's Spot as fast as I can,
tripping over the fence
and landing on my knees,
the breath punched out of me.
When I reach the bank,
I rip my boots off,
leave my clothes in a pile,
and jump into the darkness,
reaching blindly for the rope.
Fingers grip and hold on
as I swing out to midstream,
the river silent below,
waiting.
The branch strains with my weight.
The strongest boy in town.

My father.
The man who went off in uniform
and came home angry, bitter,
blaming Larry and me for his failure.
No more!
I wrap my legs tight around the rope
and climb higher,
swinging harder and harder,
faster and farther,
the branch groaning.

"No more!" I scream.

Suddenly the branch splits like a rifle crack

as I'm swinging back to shore.

I let go,

my arms flapping like a hopeless boxer.

The sword grass is cold, sharp,

and it cuts my arms as I land.

His skin is my skin.

The branch floats in the water,

rope twirling behind like a snake.

How can I begin to accept all this?

EIGHT

The Miner

Mr. Butcher

The news is all across town.
Mr. Peabody, the headmaster, can't shut up.
"Brave Eddie."
He wants to make him honorary school captain.
He didn't even blink
when I handed him my resignation.
Grainger hasn't bothered to apologize
for his completely unjustified suspicions.
Frankly, I can't wait to start packing.
Any town that celebrates
the likes of Eddie Holding
is not where I want to stay.

Here's the hero now,
strolling in late to class with Sally.
I expected more from her.
Everyone stands when Holding walks to his desk.
This is too much.
"Sit down. All of you.
We only stand when an adult enters.
Not a mere boy."
Holding packs everything from the desk
into his bag.
"We're waiting, Holding."
He closes the desk,
picks up the inkwell in his big hand,
and walks toward me.

He says,

"There's a vacancy at the mine.

They offered it to me."

"Well. It's where you belong.

Out of sight, out of mind."

He plonks the inkwell hard on my desk,

leans over, and addresses me.

"Sorry to hear you're leaving, sir."

Larry Holding scoffs and waves to his brother.

Sally starts to walk out with Holding.

"Where are you going, young lady?"

The insolent girl doesn't even bother to face me.

She says,

"I'll come back when the new teacher arrives."

This town really is unbearable.

My fob watch says lunchtime.

My patience says it's over.

"This class is dismissed."

Larry

Geez, Butcher's face was a sight
as Eddie and Sally walked out.
When he gave us the afternoon off,
I was the first out the door.
I ran after Eddie
and slapped him on the back.
"Thanks, brother."
Half the town is calling Eddie a hero,
and the other half are saying the same about Dad.
Mrs. Kain didn't charge me for the milk
this morning.
She said,
"Your father did a bloody good thing, son.
How could anyone hurt that young girl?"
I should have asked for a chocolate as well.
How could Paley expect any girl
to be interested in him?
He always was a peacock,
parading round like he owned the town.
It beats me how Grainger can charge Dad
with anything but doing a public service.
Maybe my family aren't such no-hopers after all.

Sergeant Grainger

I've waited awhile to walk to the Holding place.
It's a small town,
everyone knew the truth
well before the *Guardian* hit the streets.
Albert is out back by his woodpile.
He stands to meet me.
"I've chopped enough for a few winters."
He almost smiles but doesn't quite make it.
"How many clues did you need, Sarge?
Before you twigged."
All night I looked through my books
searching, and finding, a lesser charge.
I've tried kidding myself it's for Albert.
And Eddie.
But, really,
it's because I'm guilty
of not doing my job quick enough.
"You ever think of trusting somebody, Albert?"
A man died and he had a hand in it.
Albert shrugs and says,
"Did you read the paper, Sarge?"
It doesn't change anything and he knows it.
"What's a fair price, Albert,
for Fatty being drunk
and having tickets on himself with a young girl?"
He drops the ax at his feet.
"I was looking for someone to blame.

Fatty got in the way."

He takes a deep, slow breath.

My hand rests on his shoulder.

"There's talk of the miners

raising bail for you, Albert."

He shakes his head,

"Tell 'em to give the money

to the O'Connors instead."

He reaches down to pick up a stack of firewood

and starts to carry it inside.

"I'll just be a minute with the wife."

I watch him walk away,

the words of Mr. Carter, last night,

echoing in my head:

If you don't look at what's in front of you,

you get overrun from behind.

Larry

When I get home early,
Mum is in the kitchen, crying.
I stand at the door
like a prize dill,
wondering what to do next.
Mum gets up and puts the kettle on.
"We spent years waiting for your father."
She leans against the bench,
her eyes wide and unblinking,
her shoulders bowed.
"And now we're going do it all again!"
She reaches for the cups,
her hands shaking.
I rush to her side
and take them from her,
placing them on the table.
"Steady on, Mum.
We've only got one set of crockery, you know."

When I'm forced to write an essay,
it's easy enough to fill a page
with some bullshit story.
And, unlike my brother,
I used homework as an excuse
for getting out of just about everything—
the washing up,
the wood-splitting,

fishing for dinner.
That can't keep happening.
Not if the old man gets put away.
Bloody hell.
He deserves a medal,
not jail.

I make the tea for Mum
and we sit together for a while,
not saying much,
listening to the silence
without the old bastard around.
And that's when it hits me.
Dad's at the police station,
and I should be there, too.

Eddie

Larry and me sit on the fence
outside the police station.
Dad walks out beside Sergeant Grainger.
He wraps his big muscly arms
around me and squeezes.
"I'm not proud, Eddie.
There's nothing decent in what I did.
But I couldn't stand by, useless.
Not this time."

There'll be lots of time to tell him
I've left school.
I'm heading down the mine.
It's good enough for Mr. O'Connor
and all the other blokes in town.
Maybe Dad wanted to protect us,
but it's him that was scared, not me.
It's the same underground as above.
There's people you trust,
and others you don't.
Someone in the family has to work
while he's in prison.

Dad looks at Larry and offers his hand.
"Don't drink as much as me, son."
Larry shakes his head and says,
"Maybe I'll get a trade, Dad.

Something useful. Like a builder."

Larry winks at me.

"We'll need an extra room on the old dump.

The way Eddie's going,

you might have grandkids soon."

Dad smiles.

"Let's hope they don't turn out like you then."

He turns and walks back inside.

Sergeant Grainger closes the door behind him.

Eddie

Sally and me walk
the long way back to her house.
Her parents let her stay out late,
just for tonight.
We walk down Main Street,
past the *Guardian*,
where Mr. Carter is sitting outside
sipping his tea.
"I'm just admiring the quiet of this street
when it rains softly."
He smiles as he sees us holding hands.
"Just imagine I'm not even here.
And Eddie, tomorrow,
if you have time,
I owe you a milkshake."
I nod in answer as he wishes us a good-night.

We stop at the end of Sally's street
so we can kiss longer,
sure her parents are still awake,
waiting for her.
I reach into my pocket
and pull out the necklace.
It shines in the streetlight
as Sally clasps it around her neck.
"I found it ages ago,
in a field beside the tracks."

She touches the locket quickly,
then puts her hands on her hips.
"It's secondhand?
Someone's castoff!"
She pretends to pull it off
and throw it over her shoulder.
"Is this what you think of me?"
I stammer, "Sally?"
She puts her arms around my neck and laughs.
"I'm joking, you boofhead.
It's beautiful.
And now it's mine."
We walk down her street
and kiss again at her gate.

Tomorrow is my first day down the mine,
but I can't go home yet.
So I walk to Taylors Bend
and sit in the grass
with the light rain brushing my skin.
This is the place where Colleen sat
the day I dive-bombed the beach.
That's how I'm going to remember her,
laughing and waving
at big old Eddie
acting the fool.

F
HER

Herrick, Steven.

Cold skin.

$18.95

711743

DATE			
11-2-11			
11-17-11			
12/5/11			
12/13/11			
1-6-12			